A CASE of DEATH
In Disguise

Texas General Cozy Cases
Of Mystery
Book 2

BECKI WILLIS

Copyright © 2020 Becki Willis

All rights reserved. No part of this book may be copied, shared, or reproduced without written consent of the author. This is a work of fiction. All characters, businesses, and interaction with these people and places are purely fictional and a figment of the writer's imagination. Locales and public names are sometimes used for atmospheric purposes only.

Cover Design by Anelia Savova (annrsdesign.com)

Editing by SJS Editorial Services

Special thanks to Casey Willis, RN for Medical Terminology Consultation

ISBN: 978-0-9987902-6-8

TABLE OF CONTENTS

CHAPTER ONE 1
CHAPTER TWO 10
CHAPTER THREE 21
CHAPTER FOUR 30
CHAPTER FIVE 39
CHAPTER SIX 47
CHAPTER SEVEN 59
CHAPTER EIGHT 73
CHAPTER NINE 90
CHAPTER TEN 105
CHAPTER ELEVEN 116
CHAPTER TWELVE 129
CHAPTER THIRTEEN 142
ABOUT THE AUTHOR 152

CHAPTER ONE

"Shanae, we may need to keep an eye on those two in Room 1."

Laurel Benson made the comment from the side of her mouth as she slipped into the nurse's station.

Her friend looked at her in surprise. "The two old ladies?"

Laurel winced at her wording. "Don't let them hear you call them that. I have a feeling they would take exception to the word 'old.'"

"They're both eighty, if they're a day!" Shanae Burns insisted.

"I know that. And *they* know that. But I don't think they like calling attention to the fact."

"I don't like calling attention to the fact I'm overweight and underpaid," her friend muttered half-beneath her breath, "but facts are facts. But fine. I'll play along." She batted her dark eyes with exaggerated innocence. "Why do we need to keep an eye on the two youngsters in Room 1?"

Laurel darted her gaze toward the Game Day table. Today was the last home game of Aggie Football, a near-sacred event at Texas A & M University. The institute of higher learning was well known for their Twelfth Man spirit and their legendary tailgate parties. Keeping with the time-honored tradition, Texas General Hospital hosted its own version of healthy snacking on Game Day.

Behind the swinging doors of each department, however, another competition brewed. These versions of game day offerings had more to do with high caloric intake and sumptuous cuisine than they did with healthy options. They even had a trophy of their own to vie for, a massive maroon and white wreath that moved from one winning station to the next.

The Game Day table in the Emergency Room station, Laurel noted, had become decidedly lighter since the women's arrival.

"I'm not accusing them," she claimed, though simply bringing attention to the fact said otherwise, "but between the two of them, they've gone to the restroom at least five times."

Her friend was unimpressed. "My old granny can't hold her bladder, neither."

"But the patient, the one hobbling around with a hurt ankle, has gone three of those times. She happens to be in one of the few rooms that doesn't have a private bath. I told her there was a restroom right around the corner from her room, but she insists on limping all the way up here, to use this one." Laurel inclined her dark curls to the restroom in question. "Conveniently located, you may notice, directly across from the table."

"Is the patient the tall, skinny one or the short, round one?"

The scowl on Laurel's face spoke volumes. She compromised with, "She's the heavier of the two."

Turning to inspect the table, it was Shanae's turn to scowl. "There was a full platter of spicy wings, not ten minutes ago. Now it's almost empty!"

Laurel's smile was triumphant. "I rest my case."

"I haven't even had time for a second plate," Shanae grumbled. "The Fandemoniums will be here anytime now, and I'm already worn out and half-starved, to boot. And to make matters worse, I just saw Captain Courageous come back a few minutes ago."

"Cade's here?" Laurel asked in a squeaky voice. At her co-worker's sharp look, she cleared the frog from her throat, willed her heart to a steady thump, and asked in a much more sedate tone, "Do you mean Detective Resnick?"

"No, I mean Captain Courageous. Red leotards, blue cape, star-shaped mask. They just put him in Room 4." Her pearly whites shone when she teased, "So. It's *Cade* now, is it?"

Laurel brushed the comment away with barely a blush. "Never mind that. What's with the costume? Halloween is over."

Another flash of white teeth. "You tell me. He's your patient."

Fandemonium was the term they had coined for the added influx of patients on Game Days. Saturdays were always busy in the ER, but toss in tens of thousands of football fans, and things quickly became chaotic. It was just as well that her friend hadn't been referring to College Station Detective Cade Resnick. Game Days were crazy enough, without the handsome police officer added into the mix. Laurel didn't have time for the highly maddening, extremely distracting, blond-haired hero.

As she pulled aside the curtain and stepped into Room 4, she decided she didn't have time for a gray-haired, costume-clad hero, either.

After a six-year tenure in the trauma department of

one of Houston's busiest hospitals, Laurel was adept at assessing patients in a single glance. Adult male. Five-foot-ten. Taller, if he weren't so stooped. A hundred and seventy pounds, tops. Poor muscle tone. Age spots on his hands. Much too old to be playing dress-up, though the tights are probably good for his circulation. No obvious signs of trauma, but it's hard to know without seeing his face. Eyes look bloodshot, but could be the red star cutouts. Hmm. When did superheroes start wearing feathery, pink, high-heeled slippers? And that protrusion in his... Good grief! Now I see why he's stooped over. How many little blue pills did this man take?

Managing to find her voice, Laurel roused a smile—*poor choice of words*—to go with it. "Hello. I'm Laurel, and I'll be your nurse today. And you are?"

"You can call me Captain," came the sullen answer from behind the mask.

"Sorry. I need a name—and a face—before I can treat you." She glanced down at the paperwork with the suspiciously empty lines. "Did they not ask you for your name in admissions?" Her tone was perplexed.

"They asked," he admitted with reluctance. "I just didn't give it to them."

There had to be a reason for the oversight. Even before he peeled away the mask, Laurel suspected it was more of a powerplay than an oversight.

"This doesn't go beyond this room," he warned, his face still averted. "I'm paying cash. No insurance. I instructed them to put me down as John Doe." His voice turned defiant. "It's your word against mine."

Except, of course, that everyone knew who he was.

This was the renowned Dr. Arnold Fisk, CEO at the largest hospital in the area, and *Texas General's* most vocal rival.

And he just happened to be married to the College Station Assistant Chief of Police Corinda Addison-Fisk.

Finally free of the pompous doctor, Laurel took a moment to collect herself before moving to the next room.

It's true, she thought. Doctors make the worst patients of all. But if he didn't want to call attention to himself, he shouldn't have shown up in a superhero costume and fuzzy slippers!

She hadn't asked about the clothes. Maybe he was wearing them at the time of the incident (it wasn't her place to judge) or maybe he had changed into them to keep his identity secret. But the slippers? The pink fur just didn't jive with the superhero persona. He mumbled something about an ingrown toenail, followed by a stern lecture on patient/caregiver confidentiality.

Shaking the long and lingering list of HIPAA quotes from her head, Laurel hoped the visual images would soon follow. *That* wasn't the image she wanted in her mind associated with superheroes. Quite deliberately, she brought Cade Resnick's image to mind. Maybe if she concentrated on the detective known to wear spurs and scuffed boots, she could erase the sight of a skin-tight bodysuit from her memory banks.

It was worth the try.

"Mrs. Shanks?" she called the greeting before she pulled aside the curtain and entered the cubicle.

"Wanda had to go to the little girl's room," her companion explained.

"Again?" Laurel frowned. "Does she have a condition

we should know about? A urinary tract infection, perhaps? We could help her with that." *And save what's left of the Game Day table.*

"No," the tall woman said with a heavy sigh. "She just can't hold her margaritas."

Laurel studied the woman before her. Something about her struck a chord in her memory. The same memory trying so valiantly to forget the man in the previous room.

"Have you been here before?" Laurel asked. "You look familiar."

"I just have that sort of face," the woman answered.

"Don't let her fool you." The voice came from behind them as the patient returned.

Laurel caught a faint whiff of jalapenos and bacon when Wanda Shanks waddled past on her swollen ankle, purse in tow. A very full, heavy-looking purse. The nurse gave a forlorn thought to the peanut butter brownies she had yet to try. Those were probably in the purse, alongside the rest of the jalapeno poppers.

"You probably recognize her from television," Mrs. Shanks continued, "or from the newspapers when she retired. The Sisters threw one whopper of a party when she finally hung up her robes."

"I was justice of the peace for River County and mayor of Juliet. I didn't wear a robe," the thinner of the women scoffed.

Too bad Dr. Fisk didn't throw on a robe while he was putting on his slippers.

Laurel gave herself a stern mental shake. *Stop thinking about Dr. Fisk!*

"She's being unusually modest," Wanda Shanks insisted. She brightened as a thought occurred to her. "Say! Do you offer celebrity discounts?"

"Your friend's not the patient," Laurel reminded her. As recognition dawned, a smile lit her face. "You're Granny Bert!" she said to the friend. "From that reality makeover show, *Home Again*. You gave that old mansion to your granddaughter."

Bertha Cessna held up a wrinkled hand. "Don't get that rumor started. I have six grandchildren. I can't be playing favorites and give one a house, and not the others. I sold it to her, fair and square."

"And they remodeled it on-air." Laurel remembered it now. "They devoted the entire season to it. She's some sort of private investigator. And she has the best friend with the restaurant and the sexy firefighter guy."

"Maddy's not really a PI," Granny Bert corrected, "but she has trouble convincing her clients of that. She owns *In a Pinch Temporary Services*. I'm trying to convince her to get a PI license so we can go in business together, but Brash isn't too keen on the idea."

"Ah, that's right." Laurel smiled, thinking of the behind-the-scenes romance that played out on live television. "Brash deCordova, the chief of police." Before her mind could drift to another assistant chief of police, Laurel put it from her mind. "I enjoyed watching the show." She deliberately turned and addressed her patient. "I have good news for you, Mrs. Shanks. It looks like your ankle isn't broken, after all. Dr. Luna will be in shortly with all the details."

"Praise Jesus!" the heavy-set woman said, placing her purse into a nearby chair with care.

That was *definitely* the scent of bacon wafting through the air.

"I told you it wasn't broken," Granny Bert told her friend with a sniff. "You just had too many margaritas and lost your balance. Maybe next time you won't guzzle those drinks like they're water."

"But it was two-for-one happy hour," Wanda whined. "I wanted to get my money's worth."

"Four margaritas are clearly too many, especially with your pea-sized bladder." A sudden smile pushed a wave of wrinkles across her face. "Pun intended."

Ignoring the reference to her drinking, Wanda changed the subject. "You'll never believe who I just saw."

Uh-oh, Laurel thought. Here it comes.

"Mabel Crowder," the woman said, instead. "She's on the other side of the hall, carrying on about something awful with her stomach." Turning concerned eyes to the nurse, she asked, "What's wrong with our friend? She's from The Sisters, too."

Surprised by the unexpected turn of conversation, Laurel stammered, "I—I can't disclose that. Even if I knew, I couldn't divulge such information because of patient confidentiality rules."

"Good luck understanding a word she says. You may need us as an interpreter," Granny Bert warned. "Her tongue is tied tighter than a chastity belt on a nun!"

Yet another fun image for the day.

"I'd tell you about the time she called in to enter a radio contest, and they thought she was confessing to murder, but I don't have time. I want Wanda to see the guy next door before he manages to get away. Someone needs to tell him that pink slippers don't go with a Superman outfit."

"I think he's supposed to be Captain Courageous." Forgetting all about HIPAA regulations, she added, "There was something about an ingrown toenail…"

"Hmph!" Granny Bert gave an unladylike snort. "Most likely, the man couldn't bend over to tie his shoes."

More unwanted images swirled inside Laurel's head. "As I said," she said with a hasty gulp, "Dr. Luna will be right in."

They had no way of knowing that, before the day was done, Dr. Fink would return to the ER as the victim of a violent crime.

And that this time, he would be fighting for his very life.

CHAPTER TWO

Over the course of midday, a steady stream of patients came through the emergency room.
Most of their ailments were common enough, particularly for Game Day.
Too many beers vs. too many stadium steps. Severe heartburn, exacerbated by extreme amounts of brisket and sausage. Blistered hands and burned fingers, via barbecue pits and one extremely hot platter. 'Friendly' wagers turned violent by too much alcohol.
Disbursed amid the Fandemoniums were the 'on any given day' emergencies.
Deer hunter vs. tree stand. A toddler's hand stuck in a glass jar. Severe migraine. Suspected heart attack. Fender-bender with minor injuries.
Laurel was exhausted long before her shift ended.
"Keep ice on your ankle and avoid any more mock replays," she advised the patient in Room 2.
"But that was an awesome catch!" the man insisted. His left ankle was the size of his knee, but he was all smiles. Laurel suspected it had more to do with the alcohol in his system than the pain reliever they had given him. By nightfall, both would be worn off, and he would be in significant pain. "It was just like my junior year at college," he went on. "We were down by five,

and the clock was ticking. The QB dropped back to throw, but the defensive end hit him hard. The ball—"

Laurel tuned him out, the same way she had the last three times he told the story. His wife listened with what passed as enthusiasm, nodding her blonde head in all the appropriate places and offering a wide smile as he embellished the tale with wild arm movements. From his position on the bed, he couldn't see the earbuds tucked inside her diamond-studded earlobes.

Laurel could only be so lucky.

"That play today was like stepping back in time and seeing myself out on that field again," the man concluded. His eyes were glazed with memories and martinis.

Laurel wondered how many years ago that had been. His wife appeared to be a well-preserved forty and several years his junior.

"Next time, just hit rewind," Laurel advised. "It's easier than re-enacting the plays in your backyard, and much less painful. You're free to go."

As she pushed open the curtain, he insisted on having the last word. "It may be easier, but it's not nearly as much fun."

Having never been much for sports, Laurel didn't understand the mentality of athletes, but she certainly understood their passion. She felt the same about nursing.

Hearing the wail of an incoming ambulance, Laurel braced herself for the next round. Experience told her it could be anything, but it didn't prepare her for the man on the gurney.

She recognized the red and blue costume before she saw his colorless face.

Gray pallor of near death. Sunken cheeks, lax facial

muscles. Judging from all the blood, wound in chest appears to be major cause of distress. On the plus side, effects of pills have worn off.

A medic practically sat on the man's chest, valiantly performing chest compressions. *Doesn't look good for our Captain.*

Laurel rushed ahead of the gurney, preparing his room and barking out orders for more help and specific equipment.

The next forty-five minutes were touch and go. Hands and arms reached from all directions, hooking up monitors, starting IVs, drawing labs, and making every effort to stabilize the patient. It was several minutes before Laurel got a clear look at the wound.

Small, irregularly shaped puncture wound to upper left chest. Hard to tell with so much blood gushing from it but appears to be two or more inches deep.

The shape of the wound brought to mind the shape of a stiletto heel. More specifically, it reminded Laurel of the high-heeled pink slippers. Her eyes darted to his feet.

Bare.

With Fink's heart now beating on its own, chest compressions ceased, but the free-flowing blood was another matter. Laurel applied a pressure dressing. The first dressing was immediately saturated. As she discarded it for a fresh one, she was hardly surprised to see a blood-soaked feather amid the pool of red. Only a thin vein of pink was visible, but it was enough to identify the weapon.

After an agonizing flurry of activity and alarms, the danger of bleeding out lessened. Another ten minutes, and the doctor suggested Laurel take a break.

She peeled away the soiled gown and gloves the moment the words cleared his lips. She definitely needed the fresh air.

Fresh may have been ambitious. Inhaling a deep gulp of hallway tang, Lauren settled for *different.* She headed for the break room, hoping for ten minutes off her feet.

Five would do, she told herself. Long enough to stretch her back, relax her calves, and work the kinks from the taut muscles holding her neck and shoulders hostage.

She barely managed two. As she exited the restroom, her phone buzzed with a message. She was needed in Dr. Fisk's room.

"We're sending him up for surgery," Cami St. John informed her, as she and a tech prepped for transfer. "He's stabilized enough to stitch up that hole."

Laurel pitched in to help. "I don't suppose he's come to and spoken?"

"He's moaned a few times but nothing intelligible."

"Has the wife been contacted?"

The tech answered, "She's in the waiting room."

Cami nodded. "She can go up in the elevator, as long as he continues to hold stable."

From the bed, their patient moaned. A faint utterance followed. "Na-nin-na."

As his heart rate spiked, the monitor beeped an alert. Laurel ran a sharp gaze over the prostrate man, searching for signs of distress. The numbers on the monitor fluctuated as his breathing quickened. He seemed agitated. It could be from pain, or from the mention of surgery.

His lips quivered as he tried to speak, the sound more of a moan than verbalization.

"Na-nin-na."

Laurel touched his arm, hoping to calm him. "Yes, Dr. Fisk. You're doing fine. Try to relax."

He mumbled a few more indistinct sounds, mostly

whimpers, a low moan, and another jumbled, "Na-nin-na."

"Try not to talk just now, Dr. Fisk. Let's get you fixed up, and then we can visit." Laurel kept her voice steady and upbeat, knowing her show of confidence would boost his.

"Nn." It was little more than a grunt at first. The second time, he managed more force. "Na!" He tried moving but was too weak. He only managed to set off the alarms.

"Please, Dr. Fisk. Just relax. You'll be fine." Laurel stroked his arm, her voice a soothing purr above the steady bleep of the alarm. "That's it," she cooed. "She'll be here any minute. Your wife is on her way."

In response to Cami's questioning gaze, Laurel merely shook her head and continued to comfort their patient.

"It's fine, Dr. Fisk. Everything will be fine. We're right here with you. We won't leave you." Laurel motioned for Cami to offer her own reassurances.

Confused but cooperative, Cami did as requested. Not only was she one of Laurel's best friends, but she was also one of her biggest admirers, as well. She knew Laurel had a knack with her patients, somehow sensing what they meant, even when incoherent. Cringing at the sight of the leotards, she patted his leg. "That's right, Dr. Fisk. We're here with you. I'm Cami, and Laurel and Henry are here, too. We're taking excellent care of you. There's no need to worry."

"Nay."

"Yes, Dr. Fisk, we'll stay," Laurel assured him.

As he settled down, the monitor steadied. Another string of mumbled sounds and mangled words, and he drifted back into oblivion.

Cami's phone vibrated with a message. "The wife is

on her way back," she whispered.

Laurel refitted the oximeter on his finger, belatedly noticing he was minus one glove. Most likely, one of the staff had stripped him of it to accommodate the gadget.

"She's not alone," Cami added. "Detective Hot Stuff is with her." Their friend Danni had given the officer the well-suited moniker.

"Great," Laurel muttered. She had enough to worry about without the distraction of Cade Resnick.

Behind them, the curtain rustled, and three people stepped inside.

"Arnold?" A woman's voice quivered with horror. "Oh, Arnold!"

Thanks to local news sources, Laurel recognized the newcomer as the assistant chief of police. As an African-American female in authority, she was often under public scrutiny. Laurel didn't think it fair but, for whatever reason, Corinda Addison-Fisk was held to a higher standard than the men who had come before her. How did her skin color or gender impact her ability to do a good job?

In the past when Laurel had seen the assistant chief, the woman was the epitome of confidence. She always dressed impeccably, whether in uniform, tailored suits, or sequined ball gowns. The woman she knew from news conferences and newspaper clippings held her head high and her back ramrod straight.

This Corinda looked nothing like that.

Laurel's trained eye flicked over the distraught wife in quick assessment.

Posture slumped and dejected. Borderline hysterical. A strong breeze could knock her off her feet. Skin waxen and dull, lacking vibrancy. Eyes puffy and red from crying. In danger of hyperventilating. No neat coil today; hair frizzy and sticking out in odd spots atop her head. No starched and ironed wardrobe, either. Mismatched sweatsuit with stains. Remnants of a pepperoni pizza, I think?

On the plus side, Laurel noted as an afterthought, *no costume.*

Corinda's eyes landed upon the man in the bed, and her face filled with shock. The accompanying look of horror could easily be attributed to the many tubes and machines connected to her loved one. But the confusion, Laurel gandered, came from seeing the outfit her husband wore.

"Wha—What in the…?" Her voice trailed off in shock.

Laurel chanced a discreet glance at the wife's sneaker-clad feet. No more than a size eight, she guessed.

"Arnold, what on earth has happened to you?" Corinda cried. She came forward hesitantly, obviously afraid she might add to his pain if she came too close.

At the sound of her voice, Arnold Fisk roused and tried to mumble a reply, but the words were garbled. A bit of drool worked its way down his chin.

"It's okay," Laurel reassured the quietly sobbing woman. "You can come closer. Let him know you're here, and that you're rooting for him. He's about to go up for surgery."

"S—Surgery? What for?"

Laurel shot a glance to the tall, slender man at her side. Facial similarities pegged him as a relative.

"My brother Benji." Corinda offered the introduction with a distracted wave of her hand. "You may speak freely in front of him."

"Unfortunately, there's not much I can tell you. Your husband has an open wound in his chest that needs attention. I'm sure the surgeon can tell you more and discuss options once you're upstairs."

From the bed, Dr. Fisk mumbled and moaned.

Somewhat reluctantly, Laurel relinquished her spot to his wife and the brother hovering at her side. Having just promised to stay, Laurel felt as if she were abandoning her patient, but the room was already crowded. At least Cami and Henry remained in place on the other side of the bed, monitoring tubes and pressures as the family inched closer.

Corinda gingerly touched her husband's arm. She jerked away when he moaned, but Cami's glower urged her to try again.

He mumbled out a few sounds, the only distinguishable one being, "Na-nin-na."

"I'm here, Arnold," his wife whispered. "Benji and I are both here."

Instead of being comforted by her voice, he seemed agitated. He tried again to speak, his weak voice stirring to a higher pitch. "Na! Na-nin-na. Na-nin-na nun nus. Ha nun nus."

When the monitors binged in response, Cami threatened to make the family leave. Benji sank into a chair along the wall, but Corinda stood her ground, even if her demeanor was timid and meek.

Laurel would have stayed, but the detective beckoned her to join him in the corridor.

Dang it! Of course he would look as handsome and sexy as ever, she lamented silently. Too much testosterone for one man, that's for sure. Hard to stuff all that into a pair of tight, starched jeans and a baby-blue shirt. A shirt that looks like it was specifically cut to cover every inch of his sculpted muscles.

She pushed through the curtain and into the hall,

where she had a clear view of the monogrammed initials. Of course. Tailor made and monogrammed, probably to drive the buckle bunnies mad.

Laurel knew the officer liked to team rope in his spare time. She detected the decidedly manly aura of leather and sweat about him. And that was decidedly mud, or worse, on his boot heels.

Her foot tapped in aggravation. He doesn't have time to take me on that date he promised—we barely managed coffee! —but he obviously has time for his horse and rope.

The knowledge irked her more than it should have. Tired and out of sorts, Laurel was angry at herself for still being attracted to the man.

"Need I ask why you're here?" she inquired coolly.

This wasn't the first time their professions put them at odds. Her number one concern was her patients' well-being, not whether a crime had been committed. The detective was as equally passionate about his job, meaning the two of them had little in common and spent more time arguing than anything else.

Cade arched a brow at her snippy tone. He took a deep breath, bracing himself for the conflict he sensed was coming.

"One," he began, as if the list were long but obvious, "this was reported as a violent crime. I'm here to investigate that crime. And two, I'm here at the request of the patient's wife, who just happens to be my boss."

Laurel rattled her fingers in the air. "You'll need to speak with Dr. Renaldi about the nature of his injuries."

"I will," the detective assured her smoothly. "I also want your input. I understand he was stabbed in the chest?"

"He has a puncture wound, at any rate," Laurel

conceded. "The surgeons will know more once they go in and operate."

"Come on, Laurel, you can do better than that. Tell me your immediate impression."

Not that I'll ever admit it to you, she groused silently, *but my immediate impression is that you smell way too enticing when you lean in like that, sweat or not. And I am not noticing your brown eyes or the way they just slid over me like melted chocolate. Nope, not at all.*

"My immediate impression," she said aloud, ignoring her own thoughts, "is that I have a patient fighting for his life. At the moment, that is my only concern."

"And while I appreciate that concern, you realize I feel just as strongly about finding the person responsible for his condition. That's why I need your help."

"Can't it wait? There's a very good chance he may not survive surgery."

A determined light pierced the detective's gaze. "All the more reason to find the person who did this and bring them to justice. I need your cooperation, Nurse Benson."

A sigh slipped from her lips. Whenever he addressed her in her official capacity, she knew he was aggravated with her.

Movement behind him drew her eye. "I see the transfer team is here to take him up. This conversation will have to wait."

"I just need to ask—"

Laurel turned away, effectively ending their conversation.

Strictly speaking, the surgical team didn't need her help transferring him upstairs, but Cade didn't need to know that.

After years of treating patients during their worst

moments, Laurel had become adept at deciphering mumbled ramblings and incoherent babble. There were times when pain overruled logic, and their words made no sense, intellectually or phonetically. And there were times, of course, when she misunderstood a muttered word, or misconstrued one grunt for another. It was hardly an infallible science, but experience had given her insight into a patient's state of mind during times of emergency. Deciphering and translating their thoughts to physicians or loved ones was simply another way she could serve her patients. It was that 'something extra' she could do to bring comfort during the most difficult of times.

But what Arnold Fisk revealed a few moments ago still made no sense to her, and she wasn't ready to relay his words to the detective yet.

She and Cade had enough obstacles between them without placing him at odds with his boss.

CHAPTER THREE

Sometime later, Cade's voice stopped her at the door. "Laurel! Laurel, wait up."

She had managed to avoid him during the final hour of her shift. Patients still poured into the emergency room, keeping her running from one room to the next. The few times she came up for air, he was nowhere in sight. She assumed he accompanied Corinda Addison-Fisk and her brother upstairs to await the outcome of surgery. And, truthfully, she hadn't looked for him, in fear that it would come to this moment.

Yet here he was, and she had already clocked out. She didn't have the excuse of the job to avoid his questioning.

The sigh slipped out without her trying to stop it. "Yes?" she asked wearily.

"I need to speak with you."

Knowing it couldn't be avoided, Laurel nodded. But her head was slow to bob back upward, hanging there for a moment in sheer exhaustion.

"You look like you're asleep on your feet," he murmured.

She was surprised at the compassion in his voice. Even more surprised at the gentleness in his touch as he took her arm and guided her to the bench outside the door.

"I feel it. Today has been a busy one."

"I'll try not to keep you long," he promised. "I can come back tomorrow, but I'd like to hear your first impressions tonight, while they're still fresh on your mind."

Laurel rubbed fingers along her forehead, disturbing the tumble of unruly dark curls resting there. "There's nothing fresh about my mind," she contradicted. "Or any part of me, for that matter. Not after today."

"I can sympathize with that," he murmured, and she believed him. "But anything you remember may help. Anything at all."

"I can tell you that this wasn't his first visit here today."

"Really? Why was he here earlier?"

"*That*, I can't tell you." Her tone was emphatic, but she did add a small explanation. "Privacy laws."

"Meaning he was the patient then, as well," Cade murmured in understanding.

Laurel's hand did little to cover her wide yawn. "What I can tell you is that he wore the same Captain Courageous outfit then, plus a pair of fuzzy pink slippers."

Cade shook his blond head as if to clear the static from between his ears. "I'm not sure what part of that sentence to process first," he admitted. "I only caught a glimpse of him when I came into the room. I did see what looked like red pants."

"Oh, no," she corrected. "Those were tights. A one-piece, full-body leotard, complete with matching cape. And mask. He wasn't wearing the mask when he came in the second time. And one of his gloves was missing, at least there at the end."

A CASE OF DEATH IN DISGUISE

"Dare I ask about the pink slippers?"

His wince almost made her smile, but it required too much effort. "High heeled, with pink feathers," she told him. "The kind they wear in the movies, not the kind you wear in real life."

Cade rubbed his chin as he thought aloud. "Fisk is a fairly large man. They make those in his size?"

His look of horror finally elicited a bark of laughter from her. "Apparently so. They didn't go with the superhero outfit, but I suppose they were all he could find on short notice."

"Like that's something a man keeps laying around his bedroom," the detective grunted.

"They didn't belong to his wife," Laurel reasoned. "I'd say she's a size eight, at most."

Impressed with her keen sense of observation, he pursed his lips and nodded. "Anything else strike you as odd?"

"As if that wasn't enough," she muttered. She fought back another yawn. "The heels were about three inches high, just thick enough to bear the weight of someone who wears a size-twelve shoe, and slightly squared."

As exhausted as she was, Cade suspected she wouldn't go into such detail without good reason. "What are you telling me?"

"Unless I'm sorely mistaken, someone stabbed Arnold Fisk with one of those slippers."

"You're serious?"

Laurel lifted a slim shoulder in a shrug. "The size and shape of the wound were consistent with the size and shape of the heel on the slippers. The depth would be about right, as well. I came to that conclusion even before I saw the feather."

"What feather?"

"The one stuffed inside the hole in his chest. It came out along with most of his blood."

Cade muttered something beneath his breath that could have been a curse. In the middle of another yawn, Laurel didn't hear it clearly.

"But you say he wasn't wearing the slippers the second time?"

"Not in the hospital. You'll have to ask the medics about in the ambulance."

"I'll do that," he assured her. He gazed out toward the parking lot and released a deep sigh. "This case just became a lot more complicated."

"I'm surprised the press hasn't picked up on it yet."

"They have. I've already run them off twice, but I can't stop them from gathering outside the hospital doors."

Laurel winced, knowing reporters would make the difficult situation even worse.

"How's his wife holding up?" she thought to ask.

"It took her by surprise, but she pulled herself together and is handling it well."

"Do they have children?"

"A grown daughter who lives in Chicago."

"At least she has her brother with her. That's good."

"Apparently, he and her husband are best friends. He's taking it almost harder than she is."

"I'm sure her training helps."

His blank expression begged for an explanation.

"With hiding her emotions," she offered. She faked another yawn as she sulked to herself. *You should know. You hide yours all the time. One minute, I think you're interested in me. The next, I'm not so sure. And when you never called…*

The fake yawn seemed to make an impression on

him. "I can see how exhausted you are. Before you go, is there anything else you can think of that may help?"

"Nothing that can't wait until tomorrow," she hedged.

He stood and offered his hand. "I'll walk you to your car."

"That's not necessary."

"I think it is."

Too tired to argue, Laurel yawned for real and allowed him to haul her to her feet. He insisted on carrying her bag in one hand, while the other rested lightly on her back.

"Hey, speaking of television cameras…" she said.

He ducked instinctively. "Where?"

She swatted at his arm. "No, silly. Not here. I was thinking of a patient we had earlier in the day. I can't tell you about the patient herself, but I can tell you that the guest who was with her stars in an extremely popular television reality show."

"The only reality show I watch is *Bulls & Barrels*."

"Never heard of it."

For some reason, he looked surprised. "Really? It's about the rodeo circuit."

"Sorry. I prefer *Home Again*."

"Hey, is that the show about the old mansion they're redoing in River County?"

"Sure is."

"I have seen that a time or two," he admitted. "I know the chief of police there, Brash deCordova. Good, solid lawman. Good football player and coach, too."

The fresh air and jaunt across the parking lot had loosened her clenched muscles and relaxed her mood. She was certain it had nothing to do with the handsome man at her side or the warmth of his hand on her back.

Nothing to do with the amicable conversation they managed, for once. She was just weary enough to lean into him as they continued to her car.

"You know the funny grandmother on the show, Granny Bert? The one who says the first thing on her mind, even when it's not politically correct?"

He leaned closer to confide, "Don't tell Brash, but she's half the reason I watch."

Laurel lifted a skeptical brow. "I imagine Madison and Genesis are the other half of the reason," she mused with a smile.

Cade shrugged chiseled shoulders and admitted, "They are easy on the eye."

"Granny Bert came in today with a friend." Stopping as they reached her car, her mouth dropped into a scowl. "For a while there, I thought I was going to have to call you and report a theft."

He looked suitably wounded. "Granny Bert is my hero. Don't tell me she's a seeker."

She was surprised he knew hospital slang. It was a term they used on people who came in with exaggerated pain, seeking drugs.

"Not drugs," she corrected. "Let's just say that by the time they left, the Game Day table was considerably lighter, and the two of them were considerably heavier. Not to mention the patient's purse!"

The sound of his chuckle wormed inside her heart and made her feel lightheaded. Her hands fumbled with the key fob as she unlocked her door.

"I see my handiwork is still in effect," he murmured, noting that only the driver side released. Leave it to a police officer to cite the danger of unlocking both sides of the car. He had adjusted the setting for her a few weeks ago, shortly after they first met.

The walk across the parking lot had passed much too quickly. An awkward moment lingered between them as they both prolonged the inevitable.

Cade finally spoke, his voice low. "If I didn't need to get back in there," he proclaimed, hitching a finger over his shoulder, "I'd take you for that meal I owe you."

Laurel wasn't ready to let him off the hook so easily. He'd had three weeks to call, yet her phone had remained silent. Let him think she might reject such an invitation, even though nothing could be further from the truth.

"If I didn't reek of blood and worse," she quipped, "I might accept."

His smile did funny things to her already light head. He reached out to touch a stray curl as he told her, "That, and you might want to be awake for the main course. You look like you could fall asleep during the appetizer."

Afraid he had pegged the situation all too well, she attempted a light laugh. "Gee, aren't you the charmer." She wrinkled her nose as she pulled away and slid behind the steering wheel.

He deliberately leaned across her, depositing her bag into the passenger seat. Crowding into her personal space, he proved just how charming he could be. She could feel the warmth of his nearness as he murmured, "I never said you didn't look as beautiful as ever, Lovely Laurel."

The low timbre of his voice, combined with the heady scent of leather and male, swirled around her and quickened her breathing. She swallowed hard when he cupped her face with both his hands, trapping her curls beneath his calloused palms. Her heart stuttered out a crazy beat as he pressed a kiss against her temple.

"Go home and get some rest," he suggested, his voice just rough enough to hint of a real kiss yet to come. "We'll talk tomorrow."

She was disappointed when he didn't move to kiss her again, but she offered what she hoped could pass as a smile. "I hope your boss' husband makes it," she said sincerely.

His sigh was heavy as the weight of reality intruded upon their special moment. "Me, too." He pulled away and stood, closing the door between them. "Drive safe."

Backing out of the parking space, Laurel called herself a hundred kinds of fool.

Way to go, Laurel. Way to kill a mood. You were finally having a perfectly good conversation with the man, and you go and mention his boss' husband, lying at death's door. You had to go and remind him there was a crime committed. That fuzzy little warm feeling evaporated like dew on a summer sidewalk.

Her mouth turned down in a definite frown.

And to make matters worse—she shook her head at the knowledge— thanks to Detective Hot Stuff and his maddening kisses that aren't really kisses at all, I'm now wide awake!

An hour later, Laurel was soaking in the old claw-foot tub that transformed her turn-of-the-century craftsman into her own private oasis. The water was already tepid, but she refused to rush through the sacred ritual. After a long day at the hospital, soaking in the over-sized tub was the only surefire way to reduce her stress.

Her phone binged with a text message. She smiled when she saw Cade's name flash across the screen.

> *Just letting you know. Fisk pulled through, but still touch and go.*

Slinging water from her fingertip, she was careful not to drop the device as she texted him back.

> *Thanks for the update.*

Bubbles appeared on the screen.

> *Sorry had to cut things short tonight. Maybe next weekend?*

Was he finally asking her out on that date? Seriously? On the weekend she was scheduled to work?

> *I'm working next weekend. What about the next?*

The bubbles appeared. Disappeared. Appeared again.

> *I have to work that weekend.*

Laurel groaned aloud.

> *We can't win for losing!*

She smiled when she saw his reply.

> *I'm no quitter. I refuse to give up. We WILL find time for that date.*

Doing a soggy, slippery happy dance in the tub, Laurel smiled as she tapped out a reply.

> *I will hold you to that, sir.*

Only after she had dried off, dressed, and padded into the kitchen for a bite to eat did she realize he had done it again.

Her bath had relaxed her enough to make her feel drowsy, but his invitation rejuvenated her. Again.

Five o'clock would come entirely too early in the morning.

CHAPTER FOUR

Like Game Days, Sundays had their own quirky traditions. There were the occasional get-out-of-church emergencies, followed by NFL Game Day emergencies (a more mature version of Fandemonium, making it all the more pathetic), followed by end-of-the-weekend/avoid-Monday-morning emergencies. Scattered between were the serious matters, often mistaken at first as heartburn or hangover. Sundays, as a rule, were a bit slower than their predecessor.

This particular Sunday hadn't gotten the memo. After back-to-back chaos before noon, Laurel's calves were on fire. When she finally carved out a half hour for lunch break, she retreated to the nurses' lounge and rested her feet in a chair.

It was there that Cade found her, eyes closed and salad only half-eaten. He was polite enough not to mention the way her head drooped to one side and the gentle snore that hummed on the air.

He made a production of knocking, allowing her time to straighten her neck and collect her senses.

"Sorry to interrupt your lunch," he said. "Got a minute?"

Two minutes of sleep wasn't enough to bother

blinking from her eyes. Laurel glanced at her watch before replying, "Ten, tops."

"I just came down from ICU. I hear Dr. Fisk made it through the night."

Remembering why he was there, Laurel wished she had promised only five minutes of her time. She wasn't looking forward to this conversation.

"How's your boss holding together?" she asked.

"She's a strong lady. She's hanging in there." Cade pulled out a chair and settled in beside her. He wore his detective clothes today: starched jeans, white shirt, and a dark-gray western-cut suit jacket. His tone of voice completed the ensemble. "I need to ask you a few questions about yesterday."

In reply, she heaved out a heavy breath of air.

Wasting no time, Cade started the interview. "Tell me about his first visit to the ER."

"He came in for a .... personal matter."

"Why do you suppose he came here to *Texas General*, instead of visiting the hospital he manages?"

"I'm not saying this is the case, mind you," Laurel hedged, searching for a discreet way to explain the situation, "but some people may have considered his condition embarrassing. I can't speculate what his exact reasons were."

"Understood." He jotted down something in his notepad. "Was his wife with him?"

"No, just him. He didn't want to give his name or remove his mask, but I insisted."

"Mask?"

"Captain Courageous, remember?"

"I'm familiar with Batman, Spiderman, and the Incredible Hulk," Cade admitted. "But I don't remember Captain Courageous."

"I had to look it up," she confessed. "Banner Comics, early 40s. Known for his red body suit, blue cape, and a face mask in the shape of star, with cutouts for the eyes. Oh, and blue boots and gloves."

The visual image made the detective cringe. "Was Fisk trying for incognito mode?"

Laurel couldn't help but snort. "Sure. Because nobody notices a sixty-year-old man in a superhero costume."

"Where did the pink slippers come in?"

She laid open her palms. "Your guess is as good as mine."

Cade tapped out a rhythm of thought on the table. "So, he wore a disguise and went to a different hospital in hopes that no one would recognize him."

"Maybe."

He looked at her sharply. "You think not?"

"I don't know. Maybe."

His eyes narrowed in suspicion. "But you don't think so."

Laurel tried for a graceful way of explaining the situation without violating the man's privacy. "Given the nature of his... complaint," she said carefully, "I think it's possible he was wearing the costume when his... complaint... occurred."

His first inclination was to smile, but he dared not. No matter how comical it sounded, there was a man upstairs fighting for his life.

Instead, Cade cleared his throat. "I see. And how would you describe his demeanor the first time he came in?"

"Grouchy. A tad threatening."

Heat flashed in his brown eyes. She heard the thunder in his voice. "He *threatened* you?"

"Not like that. He threatened a lawsuit if word of

his... complaint... got out. He recited a long list of HIPAA guidelines and reminded me that I was bound by oath to keep his information and his identity private."

"That must have been some... complaint... he had," Cade muttered.

"You can't imagine." Laurel tried to shake the memory from her head.

"About the slippers..."

"There's not much to tell. They were totally out of character with his superhero costume, but he mumbled something about an ingrown toenail. Since that wasn't the nature of his complaint, I didn't ask further questions."

"And when he came in the second time?"

"No sign of them."

"Except for the feather in the wound," Cade reminded her. His expression edged toward hopeful. "I don't suppose you salvaged it as evidence?"

Laurel's dark curls danced about as she shook her head. "I'm sorry. It never even occurred to me. I was focused on slowing the loss of blood."

"That's okay. I put a hold on trash disposal for the ER."

"Someone is not going to like you," she predicted, pitying the poor souls who would sort through such filth.

"I'm not trying to win a popularity contest. I'm trying to find out who stabbed Arnold Fisk."

"Can you confirm that the weapon was, in fact, his shoe?"

Cade glanced toward the door, assuring himself that they were alone. "You didn't hear this from me, but it appears your initial observation was correct."

"Ouch." Laurel absently rubbed her chest, wondering

what would possess someone to carry out such an act. "That suggests a very personal kind of rage."

He arched a brow. "Are you a psychologist now?"

"No. Just observant," she reminded him smartly.

"There's the off chance this was an accident. He could have taken a hard fall onto the upturned heel."

"I suppose stranger things have happened," she agreed. An impish smile replaced the smirk. "Things like leaders of the community showing up at the ER in superhero costumes and high-heel slippers."

He obviously felt the need to defend his superior's husband. "He could belong to a local theater," Cade mused, for argument's sake. "Maybe he was playing the part of a patriotic tooth fairy."

She didn't utter a word, but her look told him how ridiculous his suggestion sounded.

Wisely moving on, he asked another question. "Was he conscious when he came in the second time?"

"In and out. Twice, he squeezed my hand when prompted, but for the most part, he was out."

"So, he never spoke? He never indicated who may have done this to him?"

This was the part she had dreaded.

Gathering her bravado in a deep breath, she admitted, "Only what he said when his wife arrived."

Cade's forehead bunched in confusion. "He didn't say a thing. He just grunted and groaned."

"Oh, he said plenty," she contradicted.

He stared at her in disbelief. "I was in that room, too, you know. He never said a sensible word."

"You never *heard* a sensible word," Laurel corrected him. "But I did."

He stared at her in disbelief. "There's no way you could have understood that mumbo jumbo."

She shrugged in disagreement. "Call it my superpower. Over the years, I've gotten rather good at reading mumbles and moans."

He may as well have called her a liar. "I don't believe you."

"Fine. Try me out."

He grunted.

"Whatever," she translated.

"That doesn't count. Of course, I'm skeptical."

"Fine. Try it again." She held up a staying hand. "Don't quote some article of law I have no hope of knowing," she warned. "At least be fair. Say something a patient might say."

He let out an indistinguishable grunt, followed by two more.

"Cold. So cold."

His frown confirmed her accuracy.

He grunted out a three-word sentence for the second test.

"Feed my dog."

A grudging light of appreciation sparked within his dark gaze. "How do you do that?"

"Far too much experience," she assured him. "I see patients at their worst. They're in pain, frightened, and often fighting for their lives. If I can't understand them, I can't help them. Sometimes, it helps me isolate and identify a specific area of pain to address. Just as importantly, sometimes it gives them emotional comfort, knowing what could very well be their final thoughts are conveyed to loved ones."

Clearly impressed, he wanted further confirmation. He mumbled out something else, his lips barely moving and his inflections flat. Most of the sounds ran together.

"You either said, 'my head hurts,' 'my hand hurts,' or

'my friend Bert.'" She pursed her lips in thought and added, "Or, since you're obviously trying to trick me, you may have mentioned something about a yurt."

"Not trying to trick you, per se," he denied. "But unless you're a mind reader, you can't always know what's on a patient's mind."

"You're right, of course. It's never a guarantee, but I usually come close. I may need to ask a couple of questions for clarification, but I can usually determine the gist of the conversation." She cocked her head. "What did you just say?"

"My head hurts."

She tried not to smirk. "I rest my case."

"Not so fast." He shot off a series of four more tests, three of which she easily passed.

He uttered a fifth statement, but the twinkle in his eyes put her on alert. It was another trick.

"Well?" he challenged. "What did I just say?"

"We both know what you said. You just want to hear me say the words."

"What were they?"

Laurel rolled her eyes and reluctantly fed his ego. "I think you're sexy."

A smirk edged the borders of his mouth. "It's about time you noticed," he teased.

Oh, I noticed. Even though she didn't say the words aloud, the smug look on his face suggested his superpower was mind reading.

Laurel made a show of checking her watch. "As much fun as this has been, your time is almost up."

The reminder effectively squelched the playfulness in Cade's dark gaze.

There you go again, she groused to herself. *Killing a mood.*

"For argument's sake, let's say you're fluent in Mumbo Jumbo." Despite her stellar performance, the detective still looked skeptical. "What is it you think he said when his wife arrived in the room?"

Laurel posed a question of her own. "Are you sure you want to know?"

"Of course. Why wouldn't I? I want to find the person who did this and make certain he or she is punished."

"Very well." She sighed before telling him what she had heard. "He said 'Na! Na-nin-na. Na-nin-na nun nus. Ha nun nus.' In my experience, that translates to 'No! Corinda. Corinda did this. She did this.'"

At first, he didn't say a word. He stared at her in disbelief. After a long beat, she felt Cade stiffen beside her. She heard the same sense of rigidness in his voice.

"This may be a good time to remind you of that oath you've taken, Nurse Benson. It goes without saying that none of *this* goes through *those* doors." He used a pointed finger to indicate *this* and *those*.

Offended, he felt it necessary to mention such a sacred trust, her own words came out frosty. "There's no need for a reminder, Detective. I'm fully aware of the trust my patients place in me. If the media gets wind of the way Dr. Fisk was dressed or the accusation he made, it won't be from me."

His jaw jutted forward. "You can't claim that was an accusation. This is nothing more than speculation on your part."

"As I just proved, I have an excellent track record," Laurel insisted. Her voice rang with confidence.

His brown gaze was intense. "That remains to be seen."

"I guess it does." Her movements jerky, she made

quick work of clearing away her lunch. "If there's nothing more, I really must get back to work."

"I do have more questions," he claimed, his voice taking on a stern note, "but that will do for now."

Did he really have more questions, or simply trying to regain lost ground? She had basically accused his boss— the assistant chief of police, no less— of attempted murder. That couldn't have sat well.

She suspected he was just being stubborn.

Well, two could play that game.

Laurel pushed away from the table and pulled herself to her full five foot, four inches. "Let me know if you have any arrestees you can't understand," she told him with a saucy smile. "I'll be happy to interpret."

After she sashayed from the room, Cade broke out into a grudging grin.

CHAPTER FIVE

Autumn was Laurel's favorite season of the year. She meant no disrespect to Christmas. It was still her favorite *time* of year. By making the distinction between time and season, both events could enjoy favorite status in her mind and in her heart.

Unlike many people who rushed from Halloween decorations to Christmas—trading spooky ghosts and evil witches for jolly St. Nick and sweet-faced angels—Laurel still took time to decorate for Thanksgiving. She had been working the first few days of November, so this was her first opportunity to refresh her fall decorations.

She had never been much for the scarier decorations of Halloween, preferring to embellish her pumpkins and scarecrows with a few playful ghosts and jack o'lanterns. Today, she plucked out the pieces specific to treat-or-treating and replaced them with turkeys, pilgrims, and decorative signs reminding her to be grateful.

Satisfied with the arrangement on her mantel and entryway table, Laurel moved her attentions to the front porch. She changed out a couple of yard stakes, added a wicker cornucopia atop the small hay bale, and traded the *It's a Boo-tiful Day* rug for one with an *Always be Thankful* sentiment. Pleased with her afternoon's efforts, she treated herself to a cup of coffee infused with pumpkin spice and a leftover Halloween treat. The treats were small, so she took more than one. That's the story she went with as she settled into the porch swing and enjoyed the crisp afternoon air.

In the Brazos Valley, autumn was more an extension of summer than it was a prelude to colder weather. Days like today were a true treat: brisk, crisp mornings flirting with the upper forties before mellowing into a warm, sunny, seventy-three degrees. In the South, the key ingredient for perfection was a slight breeze and the absence of humidity.

Today, in Laurel's mind, was perfect. She curled into the light sweater she wore and rocked gently, sipping her coffee as she admired the elm on her front lawn. It was beginning to show some glorious yellow color. Autumn foliage came later here than in the northern states and wasn't nearly as magnificent. But the Hendersons across the street had a maple that Laurel adored. Just before the winds of December rattled the leaves and wrestled them onto the ground, she knew they would offer a glimpse of ruddy foliage.

When her cell phone rang, she saw Cami's name flash across the screen. Laurel mentally ran through the ER rotations. Unless she had traded with someone, Cami was scheduled to work today. Since their line of work didn't lend itself to much idle time, she hoped there wasn't a problem at work. *Or,* she thought with a wince, *I hope they don't need me to come in.*

"Hey," she greeted her friend, asserting more optimism into her voice than she felt. "What's up?"

"I don't know if you've been on social media today…"

"Not if I can help it," Laurel quipped.

"Wellll, you may want to check it out. Someone went a little camera happy on Saturday."

As her stomach tanked, Laurel was afraid to ask. "You don't mean...?"

"Yep. Sure do," Cami replied. "We not only have photos and a brief video, we even have a meme. The pink slippers look especially lovely on repeat."

"Cade is going to go ballistic," Laurel muttered.

She heard the smirk in her friend's voice. "Funny, how the first thing you think of is Detective Hot Stuff."

Choosing to ignore the truth, Laurel changed the subject. "Do we know who leaked them?"

"Could have been anyone." She directed Laurel to the first online site. Together, they ogled the images on separate devices.

"This looks like it was shot from the parking lot," Laurel deduced.

Cami agreed. "And even though we have a strict no-posting policy for employees, we can't control what the public sees or shares."

"This is so not good." Laurel watched the meme of Dr. Fisk entering the building. The red star-studded cape flapped behind him in the wind as his feathered sandals stomped out a steady beat. Seeing the image once wasn't enough; it repeated on a stutter, ending with a comic book style *Ca-chow!*

Laurel worried her bottom lip as she studied it once more. "Do you think anyone can tell his identity from this angle?"

"Not really. But just wait until you see the next one."

Together, they studied the post by a different person.

Laurel was still optimistic. "He still has on the star mask and headpiece. I'm not sure that's very revealing." She bent over her phone for closer inspection. "Wait.

He's getting back into his car. Is that what I think it is in the windshield?"

"Yep. You can see his *Brazos Valley Methodist Hospital* parking pass quite plainly. As far as I know, the press hasn't revealed the fact that he made two trips to our ER that day, but it won't take a genius to connect the dots."

"Maybe not. There's no timestamp on the photo. Maybe they'll think it was taken on Halloween."

"We're not done," her friend assured her. "The next one is even better."

This one was a video. It was just a snippet, but there was no mistaking the cape as medics rushed the gurney through the sliding glass doors. To give viewers a better look, the maker of the video thoughtfully shared it in slow motion. The details were blurry, but there was no mistaking the blood and the superhero costume.

"*So* not good," Laurel repeated with a moan. "I'm sure his wife will intervene and have these photos taken down, as they could be considered evidence of some kind."

"Evidence of bad taste," Cami muttered. There was a hum on the line as she hesitated. Her voice sounded hesitant as she ventured to ask, "Did you find anything... odd... about his wife's visit?"

"I found the entire situation uncomfortably odd!" Laurel assured her. But she knew what her friend asked, and it reinforced her interpretation of Dr. Fisk's mumbo-jumbo.

"I know it was a terrible time for all of them. He was in excruciating pain. She was in shock. The brother-in-law was barely coherent. But as a couple, they seemed so... stiff." She quickly added, "No pun intended."

Against their better judgment, they both snickered at her unfortunate choice of words. In jobs such as theirs, they often had to search for levity, even in the gravest of situations.

"I'm serious, though. I know everyone reacts differently in traumatic situations or when they're in extreme pain, both physically and emotionally. But something about their little family felt dysfunctional."

Laurel pointed out the poor word choice this time. "Again, no pun intended."

"Maybe I should quit while I'm ahead," Cami groaned. "A patient just came in, anyway."

"Any word on Dr. Fisk's condition?"

"Not good. His status was downgraded." Instead of hanging up, Cami had one last thought to share. "Just one more thing. I know tomato and blood dry differently, but things were so busy that day. All I remember is something red. That was pizza sauce on the wife's shirt that day. *Wasn't* it?"

Laurel sat up straighter, her eyes popping wide open. "Of—Of course," she stammered. She sounded anything but certain.

"Yeah, I thought so." Her friend was no more convincing than she had been. A call button binged in the background, and she ended the call. "Gotta go, girlfriend."

Laurel wasted no time in texting Cade.

Have you been on social media today?

He replied quickly.

Not really my style. I prefer face to face.

She would love to explore more face-to-face time with the handsome detective and obtain first-hand knowledge about his *style*, but now wasn't the time. She made screen shots of the posts and sent them to him.

She was hardly surprised when her phone rang. Forgoing a polite greeting when she answered, Cade plowed in with a demanded, "Who did this? Where did these come from?"

"I have no idea."

"Where did you get them?"

"Apparently, they're all over the internet. Cami called to warn me."

"I thought the hospital had a policy in place to prevent this sort of thing!" It was almost an accusation.

"We do. For our employees. But these could have been taken by literally anyone."

She could hear the gears grinding in his mind. "The chief will go wild. Not to mention ACAF."

"Who?" She wrinkled her nose in confusion. "What?" Having never heard the term, she was stumped.

"Assistant Chief Addison-Fisk." He groaned with realization. "I need to give her a head's up. Look, I'll have to call you back." Uncharacteristically flustered, the detective hung up without another word.

Given the situation, Laurel didn't hold it against him.

With the peaceful aura of the afternoon shattered, Laurel went inside to pull the images up on her laptop. Even as distasteful as they were, she needed a bigger screen to study them. She made more screenshots and saved them to her files, suspecting they would eventually be pulled from the internet.

She was searching for additional postings when her phone rang, some thirty minutes later.

Again, Cade didn't bother with hellos. "I'm sorry about earlier." He launched right in. "I needed to warn my bosses, particularly ACAF, about the situation."

"I understand. I'll give you a pass." A hint of teasing slipped into her voice as she added, "This time."

His tone softened as well. "I also didn't thank you earlier for the head's up. I appreciate you letting me know."

"I'm sorry this has happened, Cade. But literally anyone could have taken those pictures."

"IT is tracking down the original posts now. As you can imagine, they've been shared and re-shared so many times, it's hard to know how many people actually took the pictures."

"My guess is at least five, probably six. Or more."

He seemed amused by her suggestion. "And how did you come to that conclusion, Nancy?"

She ignored the barb. He had called her this before, accusing her of playing Nancy Drew during his police investigation.

"If you'll look closely," she said, "they're taken from different angles and at different times. The meme was taken when he first arrived. It looks like someone recorded it from outside the hospital, probably near the entryway from his left. There's another photo taken from behind as he's entering, but I think it was from another camera. The coloration is different."

"Very observant," he murmured.

"I didn't see this until after I sent you the message, but I found one taken inside the waiting room. It looks like they were trying to do it as unobtrusively as possible, hence a lovely shot of some woman's nose and another person's elbow. The third one I sent was taken from one of the ER cubicles. You can probably obtain a list of everyone who checked in during the time he was there."

The same thought had occurred to him, but he was trained for such. He was impressed that she came to the same conclusions. "It won't account for any guests with them," he agreed, "but it's a start."

"There's a fifty-fifty chance the attending nurse or physician would remember a guest or their relationship to the patient. Not everyone is as memorable as Granny Bert from the television show, but there's always the occasional mama bear who makes our jobs more difficult, or the big burly husbands who faint when we give their wives a shot." Remembering the detective's own aversion to needles, she added with exaggerated innocence, "Some people just can't abide the long, spiky tip of a needle."

"Imagine that," Cade said, voice flat. She could picture the accompanying smirk on his face.

Then Laurel grinned, imaging the underlying green pallor, as well. She hoped he couldn't hear it in her voice as she returned to the subject at hand.

"I have no idea where the video came from. Few people have access and/or direct line of sight to the ambulance bay. I hate to say it," Laurel admitted, "but it's almost as if they knew to be on the lookout."

"Great," Cade muttered. "As if this doesn't already have the makings of a three-ring circus."

"How did the assistant chief take the news?"

"About like we expected. It's hard enough for her, knowing her husband is fighting for his very life. Once people make the connection, he'll be a public laughingstock."

"You did notice the parking pass in the one picture." Laurel made it a statement, not a question. "I'm surprised people haven't already started speculating."

She heard the displeasure in his voice. "They have. They just don't have enough proof to back it up yet."

"How long do you suppose it will take them?"

"Not long enough," Cade answered with a heavy sigh. "Nowhere nearly long enough."

CHAPTER SIX

Laurel tuned in to the ten o'clock news before getting ready for bed.

"We have breaking news this evening coming out of *Texas General Hospital*," the anchor announced. "We are saddened to announce that Dr. Arnold Fisk, CEO of *Brazos Valley Memorial Hospital* here in the twin cities, has succumbed to recent injuries and passed away. Dr. Fisk was admitted to *Texas General* ER on Sunday with a stab wound to his chest. After emergency surgery and round-the-clock care, he was pronounced dead just over thirty minutes ago. According to our sources, his wife of thirty-four years, Corinda Addison-Fisk, was at his side. Addison-Fisk is an assistant chief with the College Station Police Department. The couple moved to the area less than four years ago, when Fisk was hired to take the place of then-CEO Dr. Jay Hermano, who died of a sudden heart attack. We expect a press conference from both hospitals tomorrow morning, which we'll carry live here and over on our webpage." The anchor rattled off the web address, along with an initial statement of sorrow and loss from the *Memorial Hospital*.

Almost simultaneously, Laurel's phone buzzed.

You up?

Suspecting what prompted the message from Cade, she typed back,

Just heard.

Bubbles appeared on the screen.

Now I have a murder investigation on my hands.

Her heart went out to him, and to his boss.

I'm sorry. Anything I can do?

More bubbles.

Only if you remember something else from that night.

He couldn't see her, but Laurel shook her head as she typed.

Nothing. I told you everything I know.

A brief hesitation, before the bubbles appeared again as he typed.

And then some.

Was the man trying to pick a fight? Her nostrils flared as she jabbed out her message.

Sometimes, the truth is hard to hear.

His reply was swift and direct.

There's a difference in truth and speculation.

Fully outraged, she stabbed more letters on the keypad.

There's also a difference in seeking the truth and ignoring it.

He was awhile in replying, perhaps to censor an immediate and angry retort.

I deal in facts. Not speculation.

Following his lead, she took a deep breath before

replying.
You have your techniques. I have mine.
Not waiting for his rebuttal, she hastily added, *And mine are headed to bed.*
Cade didn't bother saying good night, and neither did she.
Laurel stalked off to bed, where she faced another restless night's sleep.

With another day off, Laurel had plenty of time to hear the many speculations swirling around Dr. Fisk's death. Rumors and theories ran rampant on social media. News commentators added their own spin to the dual press conferences. A sensationalist news channel out of Houston had picked up the story, adding yet more drama to what should have been a solemn and sedate occasion.

Station WXYZ had connected the dots, drawing a distinct line between the masked patient, the man on a gurney, and the death of the health care executive. Hospital personnel refused to confirm facts, but the television reporter was quick to note how the distinctive costume and telltale parking pass aligned with the video taken in the ambulance bay. She minced no words when describing the bizarre outfit and found several eyewitnesses willing to share their own descriptions and their own speculations. Most weren't flattering.

During their press conference, a spokesman for *Brazos Valley Memorial Hospital* suggested the doctor had attended a belated Halloween party, but reporters were quick to question that theory. Had his wife not gone to the so-called costume party with him? Where had the party taken place, and who else had been on the guest list? Why the fuzzy slippers? Why not boots, to keep in character with the rest of the outfit?

One plain-spoken eyewitness made a crack about said party. "It looked like he was celebrating, all right," the college-aged man scoffed. "But it looked more like a party contained to the bedroom, if you know what I mean." Although his parting statement was later cut from the reel, the first several feeds included his wince. "Man, I hope I never gotta resort to pills like that."

There were questions for both hospitals. Why hadn't his wife been with him on either visit to the ER? According to all evidence, he drove himself to and from the hospital the first time. When he came in the second time, who called for the ambulance? What weapon was used? Was the attack random or targeted? Where did the crime take place?

Specific details were blocked by the CSPD, citing an ongoing investigation. The elephant in the room was the assistant chief of police and her direct involvement to the case. When videos and posts were jerked from social media, no one doubted who pulled the strings.

When Laurel returned to work on Wednesday, the hospital was abuzz with whispers. The director had issued a strict gag order, but someone had leaked just enough information to have the sharks circling. Security officers manned the entrances, turning cameras and reporters away. The phone rang endlessly, as eager reporters attempted to get a statement concerning Dr. Fisk's visit and subsequent death.

"You should have been here yesterday," co-worker Mary Ann told her.

"It was a circus," Danni Barrington confirmed.

Laurel shook her head with a rueful frown. "I can only imagine." She put up a staying hand as a new patient arrived in Room 1. "I've got this," she offered.

Padding down the hallway, she knocked before pulling the curtain aside.

Thirty-something female, she assessed. Thin and toned beneath the too-big clothes. Unusually pale skin, sunken cheeks, dark smudges under eyes. Could be a user, but her teeth look good. No sores on face or arms. Odd choice of head covering. Reminds me of those old kerchiefs from I Love Lucy days. A smile itched at her lips as she mused, *Wonder if anyone ever wore those in real life, or just on TV?*

"Hello. I'm Laurel, and I'll be your nurse today. What brings you in, Miss... Carter?" She scanned the hospital bracelet on the woman's wrist, reading the name displayed on the handheld device.

"That's right. Tina Carter. I'm just not feeling myself today."

"Could you be a little more specific?" Laurel

wrapped the blood pressure cuff around her arm and waited for the near-perfect reading.

"I feel faint and out of sorts. A little dizzy when I stand." Tina's voice sounded wan.

"Are you having difficulty breathing?"

The patient tested her lungs and offered a tiny shrug. "Maybe a little. I feel all jittery inside."

"Do you mind if I listen to your heart and lungs?"

The woman lay back to give better access, but she suddenly seemed agitated. Laurel considered revising her assessment of drug use.

Strong, steady heartbeat. No congestion in the lungs. First impression says the woman is perfectly healthy.

"How's your appetite? Any abdominal pains?"

"I haven't been very hungry lately," the patient admitted. "I had some upsetting news this weekend, and—and I just haven't felt right since."

Ah, finally! Something that could make sense!

"Stress can do strange things to our bodies," Laurel agreed, her voice gentling.

"I'm nervous." The woman blurted out the words, as if making an announcement.

"There's really no need to be anxious, Tina. We just need to ask a few more questions and find out what's going on to make you feel this way. Have you had any falls lately?"

"No."

Laurel went through the routine questions, ending with, "Do you feel safe at home?"

"Home, yes." With a short laugh, Tina Carter

added, "Here, not so much."

Her answer surprised the nurse, and it reflected on her face. Laurel cocked her head to one side, sending dark curls dangling. "What makes you say that?"

"That bad news I mentioned. My friend came here over the weekend, and it didn't end so well for him."

Laurel expected wariness in the woman's eyes. She didn't expect an open challenge. Her back stiffened ever so slightly as she put away her stethoscope. "I'm sorry to hear that. But I want you to know we have some of the best doctors in the state, if not the entire country." She smiled in a reassuring manner. "Can I offer you anything to make you more comfortable? Another sheet, or a warm blanket?"

"A sheet will be fine."

Laurel looked through a cabinet until she found one, whirling just in time to see the patient lower her phone. It had been pointed in Laurel's direction.

A bit wary, Laurel smoothed the sheet over her patient's long legs.

"I may have caught something from my friend," Tina suggested. "Were you on duty this weekend?"

"As a matter of fact, I was. Do you know if you have any of the same symptoms your friend exhibited?"

"I don't know. Did you have anyone complaining of faintness and shortness of breath?"

"I saw many patients over the weekend.

Unfortunately, I heard that complaint more than once."

A challenging light came into the patient's eyes. "I actually wasn't short of breath until I arrived. Maybe there's something in the hospital making us sick."

Ignoring the hint of accusation in her voice, Laurel tried a smile. "That can most likely be attributed to your nerves. Don't worry. It happens to most people."

"Maybe there's some sort of cleaner you're using that's irritating our airways. Maybe there's unclean air ducts or some sort of allergen in the sheets." She pushed the recently proffered sheet aside. "Maybe that's what harmed my friend."

Laurel's patience grew thin. "I assume there was an initial problem that brought him in to begin with."

"Do you put all patients in these rooms, or do you have separate ones for those who are in serious condition? What about those who may be contagious?"

Laurel tried not to frown.

To be so nervous, she's certainly articulate. Not to mention a tad paranoid.

She made extra effort at reassuring her patient. "If we have reason to believe a patient requires quarantine, we have special accommodations for them. I don't recall anyone meeting those parameters this weekend."

"What if someone is admitted in grave condition? Do they go in these rooms?"

"If you're worried about cleanliness, the rooms are thoroughly cleansed and disinfected between patients."

Tina blinked twice. "But you just throw them in here, all together with the rest of us?" A hint of hysteria crept into her voice. "Like, someone could have died on this table?" She pulled into a sitting position, preparing to bolt.

"Please. Lie back and try to relax," Laurel urged in a soothing voice. She waited until Tina complied before offering more assurance. "When possible, we try to station our most serious patients nearest the elevator, so we can rush them up to surgery if needed."

Tina's eyes narrowed in thought. When she spoke again, she sounded more calculating than hysterical. "So, that would be the back hallway?"

Laurel's radar pinged in alert. Many patients asked questions when nervous, but this seemed more than ordinary. Her questions were direct and succinct, and often accusatory in nature. It felt more like an interrogation, with the tables turned. Laurel was the one supposed to be asking questions, not Tina.

Something's off with this patient. Come to think of it, she looks vaguely familiar...

Laurel tried placing the other woman, but nothing came to mind. Still searching her memory banks, she murmured, "Let me re-fluff that pillow for you."

As she pulled away, she noticed the smudge of a white substance on her glove. *Cocaine? Maybe she's a seeker, and I've seen her in here before.*

Pretending to push away a stray hair, Laurel discreetly sniffed her hand. *No. I think that's makeup. A very thick, very light-colored makeup.*

She discreetly scrutinized her patient again.

That unhealthy pallor in Tina's cheeks may have had a little help. Maybe the whole baggy-shirt, raggedy-head outfit is nothing but a costume. Decidedly better than Captain Courageous but a costume, nonetheless. Reporter, perhaps?

Her voice came out slightly warmer than frost. "Are there any other symptoms you'd like me to note?"

"I think we covered most of them."

"In that case, I'll let you rest. The doctor will be with you shortly."

Laurel stepped from the room and huffed out a deep and frustrated breath. *The nerve of some people! This is an ER, not a press conference!*

Back at the nurse's station, she shared her suspicions with the other nurses.

"What did you say her name was?" Danni asked.

"Tina Carter."

"That TV reporter from Houston is Catrina Carter," Mary Ann volunteered. "Maybe she used the name Tina when she checked in. Brown hair with red highlights?"

"She had it covered with an odd-looking scarf, tied at the top like she was doing heavy-duty cleaning or something."

"My grandma used to wear one of those."

"Exactly," Laurel said. "She's about fifty years

behind the times."
"Threaten her with a shot," Danni suggested. "Unless they're users, that usually does the trick."

Suspicious of the woman in Room 1, the nurses kept a watchful eye on her. Twice, they spotted her peeking from her cubicle with her cell phone poised for the best camera angle. Another time, she wandered in the hallway, supposedly looking for a restroom. Like with Wanda Shanks, the one next door wouldn't do.

The doctor found nothing wrong with Tina Carter. Her preliminary bloodwork looked normal, her vitals were good, and her symptoms were too vague to make a definitive diagnosis. He prepared discharge papers, suggesting she take it easy for the rest of the day and follow up with her primary physician.

"Looks like you're good to go," Laurel announced with a smile.

Tina looked startled. "Just like that? But... he didn't even say what was wrong with me!" she protested.

"I know it's frustrating. The good news, however," Laurel pointed out, "is that we know what's *not* wrong with you. It appears you've been blessed with good health, Ms. Carter."

She looked almost disappointed and continued to argue. "Still..."

"The doctor did suggest you make a follow-up appointment with your primary care physician and discuss further options with him or her, particularly if your symptoms persist."

Vague as they are, she added silently.

Tina huffed her displeasure. "I suppose."

Laurel pushed extra brightness into her smile. "You're free to go. And please. Make that follow-up appointment."

She stepped into the hall and narrowly missed colliding with the traffic there, as an aide from admissions led two women into the cubicle two doors down. There was no doubt about which was the patient, which was the guest.

Corinda Addison-Fisk leaned heavily into her companion, a large woman with a neck lanyard identifying her employment with *Brazos Valley Methodist*. Both women wore business attire and grim expressions, but Laurel couldn't help but notice how the assistant chief's face was as peaked and frail as it had been on Saturday night.

And she certainly didn't miss how Tina Carter was there to capture it all on her cell phone.

CHAPTER SEVEN

Even if the assistant chief weren't on her side of the ER—the nurses generally divided their workload by the geographical layout of the emergency department— Laurel would have requested attending the new widow. The pre-determined room assignment seemed destined by fate.

After logging into the computer and checking the patient's initial chart, Laurel knocked before entering the room.

"Hello, Mrs. Fisk," she greeted her. "I'm Laurel, and I'll be taking care of you today."

Corinda Fisk offered a half-smile in return. She obviously didn't remember the nurse, and Laurel wasn't about to remind her of their first encounter.

As she electronically scanned her patient bracelet, Laurel made her initial assessment. Appears weak and on verge of passing out. Possible danger of hyperventilating. Sweaty brow and nervous gestures. Could indicate a panic attack. In sharp contrast from her last visit, smartly dressed in what could be a uniform, what could be a plain navy skirt and jacket. Hair tidy and proper in its customary coil. Only thing out of place is the woman, herself. Her husband and her companion are both affiliated with a different hospital, so why come here?

Laurel glanced at the companion. Fifty-eight-ish. Bleached blonde over gray, pulled back so tight, her eyes are bugged and grimacing like she just sucked a lemon. Could be a naturally sour personality. Wears clothes one size too small for her tall frame, especially in the bust. Close to six feet tall. Her gaze dropped to the other woman's feet. Easily a size eleven. Or larger.

Laurel curtailed speculating as she asked, "What brings you in today, Mrs. Fisk?"

"I—I think I'm having a heart attack!"

Seated in the chair beside her, the tall woman rolled her eyes. If possible, her expression soured even more.

"Tell me more about your symptoms while I get you hooked up to the monitors. Can we speak freely in front of your friend?"

Corinda darted a nervous glance at the other woman. "We're not close friends, but Rita was kind enough to bring me here. She can stay if she likes."

Seeing a way out, Rita shot to her feet. "Maybe you'd be more comfortable if I waited in the waiting room," she offered hopefully.

"Just a moment, please." Laurel stopped her before she made her hasty retreat. "I'd like to hear her symptoms, and if you have anything to add before you go."

"I started feeling lightheaded," Corinda recalled.

"My breath was shallow at first, and then fast and furious. My heart was racing, my mind was spinning, and I broke out in a cold sweat. I thought I might lose my breakfast. Or pass out. Or both."

"Were you standing when this happened? Bending over, perhaps?"

Recalling the sequence of events, Corinda struggled to get out a single word. "S—S—Sitting." It was all she could manage, so the woman called Rita filled in the rest.

"I'm Rita Bernard, Dr. Fisk's administrative assistant," she volunteered. "I opened his office for her this afternoon, so she could clear out his things."

"So, you haven't eaten since breakfast?" Laurel inquired, getting a clearer picture of the situation.

Throw low blood sugar, emotional distress, and physical exhaustion into the mix, and you have the makings for the perfect storm.

"Is there anything else you can offer, Ms. Bernard?" she asked the antsy woman. Clearly, the bleached blonde was eager to leave.

"Like all of us who knew Dr. Fisk, Mrs. Fisk is understandably distraught." Her words were as stiff and formal as her lemon-faced demeanor. "I tried to tell her it was too soon to clear out his office, but she insisted. I think it was too overwhelming, seeing his personal effects."

Crying softly into her hands, the newly proclaimed widow nodded her head.

"Thank you, Ms. Bernard. If you aren't sure on how to return to the waiting room, stop by the nurse's station, and they'll be happy to direct you."

"If I can find my way around *Methodist*, I can surely find my way around *here*." Her voice dripped with disdain.

Laurel felt a stab of sympathy for the late doctor, knowing he had to work closely with the dour woman.

She couldn't help a parting glance at the woman's disappearing size elevens. *As tall as she is now, I wonder if she ever wears stilettos?*

She turned back to her patient, focusing her attention there. "Are you experiencing any pressure in your chest? Any pain in your right jaw, arm, or shoulder?"

Brushing away the tears and sniffing, Corinda shook her head no.

"I'm sorry," she said, her words thick with recent tears.

"There's nothing to be sorry about, Mrs. Fisk." Laurel's voice was gentle and reassuring. "You've been through a terrible ordeal and suffered a tremendous loss. It's perfectly normal to be emotional. And it's also perfectly normal to experience a panic attack at times like these. Can you tell me more about your actions leading up to the event? Had you walked a long distance, for instance, or taken the stairs? Were you breathing normally before you were seated at the desk?"

She shook her head to the contrary. "Just walking into his office took my breath away. I—I still can't believe he's gone. He spent so much time at that

A CASE OF DEATH IN DISGUISE

damn office, I half-expected to find him there still, buried beneath a pile of paperwork!"

The venomous tone in her voice surprised Laurel. *Must have been trouble in paradise,* she mused.

Aloud, she said, "I imagine a job like his did demand a lot of time away from home. As does yours."

"We lead—*led*—busy lives, but we were both driven to be the best at what we did."

"Had you been married long?"

"Almost thirty-five years. Being an interracial couple in the 80s was difficult enough without the pressure of our careers, but we made it work."

Laurel asked routine questions about Corinda's general health and any family history of heart issues. The more the police chief talked, the calmer she became. Her pulse and breathing stabilized, and a bit of color seeped back into her sallow cheeks. Her vitals reinforced Laurel's initial assessment of a panic attack, but the doctor would be the one to make a formal diagnosis. Protocol demanded they run preliminary tests to rule out a heart attack.

As the conversation came full circle, Laurel asked about events immediately preceding her episode. "What were you doing when you first felt your symptoms?"

A shadow descended over her face and clouded her dark eyes. "I was looking through Arnold's desk. Seeing his handwriting…" Her voice trailed off before she finished with a weak, "Let's just say… it threw me for a loop."

"I'm sure it was difficult," she murmured, not without empathy. Even if she suspected there was more to their story than met the eye, the woman had lost her husband and the father of her child. Angry with him or not, she was suffering.

Had she been angry enough to kill him? I get the distinct impression they hadn't been happy there at the last, Laurel mused. And I can't forget what he said. He said Corinda did this to him.

Maybe, she further mused, she discovered him having an affair with sour-faced Rita and used one of her size twelves to stab him in the heart. A crime of passion which now she regrets because she truly did love her husband.

More than once, people had accused Laurel of being a romantic at heart.

Not, she noted, that it had done much for her own love life. In fact, as her friends and her mother often pointed out, perhaps it was her idyllic and unrealistic notions of love and romance that kept her from finding a suitable man. Kenton had been a poor example of what *suitable* equated to. Just because he was in the medical profession and they shared a career, didn't mean they shared core values and respect for one another. His cheating on her—multiple times, with multiple women—was a perfect example of his lack of respect for her and their relationship.

Breaking their engagement and returning to her roots was Laurel's first step toward regaining her self-respect and rebuilding her confidence, but it had quickly taken a backseat to her workload. She hadn't *meant* to bury herself in her career, but at the end of a long, stressful day, the last thing on her mind was starting a new relationship. In fact, until she met a certain police detective, she had absolutely no interest in dating again.

Then along came a pair of velvety brown eyes, long legs encased in starched, faded denim, and a maddening smirk that set her heart to jingling as surely as his spurs, and the balance in her world shifted. She was still as tired as ever, but a new sense of restlessness stirred in her blood.

The trouble was, neither she nor Cade had the time or luxury to see where the jingle of her heart might lead.

Pulling her mind back on track, Laurel reminded herself that her own love life (or lack thereof) was of no concern right now. Guilty or not of her husband's murder, Corinda Addison-Fisk was in danger, however slight, of having a legitimate heart condition. It deserved her full attention.

Satisfied with the readings she saw on the monitors, Laurel began undoing them. "I'm sure the doctor will call for tests, so you may want to change into a hospital gown for ease of access. Once you're changed, press the call button, and I'll be in to hook you back up." She pulled a gown and an extra blanket from the overhead cabinets and laid them on the bed. "Is there anything else I can do for you?"

"Turn back the clock," her patient muttered. "Two years should do the trick."

Laurel expected her to say Saturday. Did that mean the couple had been having marital issues for the past two years? Was that when it all started to go wrong?

Not my place to judge, she reminded herself. Just to heal.

"It would be an awesome superpower, wouldn't it?" Laurel mused aloud. "We could solve so many problems, if only we could see into the future or go back into the past. Unfortunately, all we have to work with is the present."

Corinda grunted in agreement, her eyes filled with sadness and regret.

"Just hit that call button when you're done," Laurel reminded her as she exited the room.

Stepping into the hallway, she was surprised to see Rita Bernard still there. Even more surprising was who was with her. Tina Carter.

"This can't be good," Laurel muttered. The two women were huddled together near the exit, their voices hushed, and their expressions animated. With everyone else busy inside patients' rooms, they hadn't bothered to step beyond the doors to talk. *That*, Laurel determined, *was about to change.*

Rita looked up and caught a glimpse of Laurel's frown. Long before the nurse could march their way, she made a hasty exit.

Laurel didn't have time to see if Tina followed suit. The wail of a siren drew her attention as the ambulance bay doors slid open and more chaos arrived.

Coming from a patient room down the opposite corridor, Mary Ann saw Laurel and called, "On it!"

Laurel had just enough time to check in with another patient before the call light lit up in Room 3. Heading back to Mrs. Fisk's room, she caught a glimpse of a familiar kerchief and baggy t-shirt lurking around the corner.

She marched right past Room 3 and practically chased Tina Carter down. It was amazing how fast her short legs could travel when fueled with indignation.

When she got within a few feet of the wandering woman, she called her name sharply.

Tina turned with a sheepish expression on her face. "I was confused on which hall to take," she offered lamely.

Laurel's reply was dry. "I suppose you missed the flashing Exit sign when you were standing beside it a moment ago."

"You know what they say. Can't see what's right in front of your own face." Tina waved a hand in demonstration, but all Laurel noticed was that some of her makeup was smudged, allowing her natural complexion to show through. It looked amazingly healthy.

"Allow me to show you out," she offered frostily.

"That won't be necessary. I know the way now," Tina chirped.

"I insist. It will give me the chance to remind you that anything you saw or heard while here in our hospital is strictly confidential." She seared the woman with a sizzling gaze. "I doubt your producer, nor the television station would relish a lawsuit over illegally obtained material." In truth, she wasn't sure the hospital could take any such action, but the important thing was to get in her bluff.

It seemed to work. Tina had the grace to look chagrined.

"You know who I am?" She fidgeted under the nurse's hazel beam.

"I do. And the photos you took today had better not show up on any form of media, or I'll lodge a formal complaint against you *and* the station."

"What—What photos?" the reporter asked innocently.

"Hand me your phone, and I'll show you." Laurel's challenge came with a deceptively sweet smile.

Tina's attitude did an about-face. "Like that's going to happen. The public has a right to know what's going on. For all we know, there's a serial killer running rampant, right here in Bryan-College Station."

Laurel's reply to the wild accusation was calm but firm. "A single incident does not a serial killer make. You have your release papers. If you refuse to leave, I'm afraid I'll have to call security."

"I'm going," Catrina "Tina" Carter spat. "But you haven't seen the last of me."

"I can get a restraining order that says otherwise," Laurel assured the pesky woman. "Good day, Ms. Carter."

She pushed the exit open, making certain the doors closed behind the reporter before she retraced her steps to Corinda Fisk's room, or ACAF, in Cade's terms. As soon as she had the chance, she would call the detective and report the incident with WXYZ's troublesome reporter.

A surge of compassion swept through Laurel as she considered the grief the assistant chief would face from the media. Sensationalist reporters like Catrina Carter had no sympathy for any aftermath their havoc might create. They were only interested in a story, and the juicier, the better. They would dig until they found something to exploit, no matter how small or how irrelevant.

Putting extra brightness into her smile, Laurel entered the room. "How about we get you hooked back up and find out what's causing your troubles? Sound like a plan?"

The patient's weak smile didn't match hers. "I suppose."

"Are you still experiencing any of the symptoms? Shortness of breath? Racing heart? Any dizziness at all?"

"I seem to be better now. As long as..." She closed her eyes briefly, perhaps to gather strength. "As long as I don't remember."

"Remember?" Though curious, Laurel forced herself to offer only a prompt. If Corinda wanted to talk, she would listen.

"How I brought him here. It was my idea. My fault."

Is this a confession? Should I call Cade? Laurel's mind swirled with questions. Indecision made her clumsy. She had trouble fitting the blood pressure cuff around Corinda's arm.

Oblivious to Laurel's suspicions, her patient continued to ramble, "I keep remembering that night. There was too much blood. This—This wasn't supposed to happen. But when I found him there... with the shoe..."

In spite of herself, Laurel gasped. "*You* found him? With the shoes?"

"Just the one," Corinda murmured. Her eyes were glazed over, as if she heard Laurel speaking but wasn't aware she was in the room. "It was—It was—" She struggled with the sentence, wailing by the time she finished. "It was shoved into his chest!"

Did that mean she wasn't the one to put it there? Or had she done it in a blind rage and then been shocked by the reality of her actions? Had the shoe belonged to Rita Bernard? Laurel wasn't sure, but she was certain about one thing. The woman's anguish was real. And was gearing up for another panic attack.

With Mrs. Fisk back in mild respiratory distress, Laurel spoke to her reassuringly.

"What's your favorite flower, Mrs. Fisk?"

"R—Roses. Arnold," she gasped between quick, hard breaths, "Arnold gave them to me every— every birthday and—and every anniversary."

"Okay, I want you to imagine taking in a deep breath. You're inhaling the beautiful fragrance of the roses. Breathe it in, deeply and slowly. That's right. Now, I want you to image you're blowing out the candles on your birthday cake. A quick, fast breath. There you go. Again. Smmmell the roses," she pulled the words slowly out, before the pace increased sharply, "then blow out that candle! And again. Smmmell the roses, blow out the candle. Smmmell the roses, blow out the candle."

By the time she practiced the breathing exercises a dozen times, her panic attack had subsided, and the doctor came into the room.

"Hello, Mrs. Fisk. I'm Dr. Sherwood." The attractive brunette smiled warmly at her patient. "I understand you're having some troubles this afternoon. Care to tell me more about what's going on?"

After listening to her halting answers, the doctor called for more tests, just as Laurel suspected. While the technicians drew blood, took images and an EKG, and basically monopolized the patient for the time being, Laurel slipped away to attend to other patients and to make an important call.

She got Cade's answering machine, but she left a message.

"Cade, I have something I need to talk with you about. I think it could be important. Call me as soon as you get this message."

Belatedly, she realized she hadn't left her name. She hoped he had her name and number programmed in his phone, but she knew he was a busy man and fielded scores of calls each day. Just to be certain, she dialed his number a second time.

"This is Laurel. I just left you a message, but I forgot to say who was calling. In case you didn't recognize my voice." Laurel cringed as the words left her mouth. *Could she sound any more pathetic?* She sounded like an awkward schoolgirl, calling her crush. "Anyway, I think it could be urgent. Call me back."

As she hung up, Laurel hung her head in shame. Was she so inept at calling men that now she couldn't even report hearing a potential confession to murder?

Pathetic, she decided. I'm pathetic.

It was her initial assessment, but she was sticking to it.

CHAPTER EIGHT

Cade didn't call that evening.

He didn't call the next morning.

It was midday before he finally returned her call.

So much for *urgent*.

The first thing he said was, "I'm sorry I haven't called before now. It's been murder around here." After a brief pause and an imagined wince, he added, "No pun intended. Bad choice of words."

"I understand. And I wholeheartedly agree. I'm sorry, but I can't talk. We're getting slammed."

"Rainy days will do that," he agreed. "Think you can find time to grab a bite after work?"

Laurel was too busy to worry this might be the 'date' he often alluded to.

"If I'm still coherent," she answered. "I'll text you. I really do have to go."

"Later."

It was late into the afternoon before Laurel took a decent break and finally ate her lunch.

"What a day," she groaned.

"I hear you, sister," Danni commiserated. "On days like this, I wonder what I was thinking, wanting to become a nurse."

"Like me, you wanted to make a difference." Laurel spoke with her eyes closed and her head tilted back. It was a poor substitute for sleep, but the best she could do in fifteen minutes.

"Surely, there's an easier way," Danni muttered.

After a lapse of several minutes—did Laurel hear a soft snore? —Danni spoke again, startling Laurel from her relaxed posture. Maybe the snore had been her own.

"Hey! Are you free Saturday night? Remember my friend Gunny?"

Laurel groaned. "Please don't set me up on another semi-blind date. You know how much I hate those."

"I'm not suggesting a date." Danni pulled a face, which quickly morphed into a smile. "Although, that's not a bad idea…"

"No. No. And no." She used a different inflection for each repeat of the word. "Also a no on being free. I'm scheduled to work all weekend."

"Too bad. I wanted you to go to The Chicken with me."

Laurel groaned. "I thought we outgrew that phase in the last decade."

Dimples appeared as Danni's smile widened. "Does one *ever* really outgrow The Dixie Chicken? It's a Brazos Valley tradition. And it just so happens Gunny and his band are playing there Saturday night."

"That would be the only reason I stepped foot in

a bar again," Laurel muttered.

"Come on, Laurel. It will be fun. We don't have to stay late, just until he finishes his set. We'll be out by midnight."

"I'll be out, all right. Passed out asleep in my bed!"

"Don't be such an old woman," Danni taunted. "Live a little."

"Don't try to bully me. It won't work."

Wagging her rust-colored brows, Danni changed her tactics. "He's really good, you know. But if you prefer, I can arrange for a private concert. Just the two of you."

"No, I don't prefer."

"Great! What time shall I pick you up Saturday night? Maybe Cami can join us."

Saved by the bell, Laurel grabbed her phone. "I'll ask. This is her calling." She deliberately turned her back on her gloating friend. They both knew that sooner or later, Danni would wear her down, and she would eventually say yes. It was easier to do without sleep than it was to endure a needling, whining Danni. "Hey, Cami. What's up?"

"I just turned on the TV. There's a breaking news story about the Fisk case."

Laurel groaned. "Do I even want to know?"

"Probably not. Guess whose favorite reporter is reporting a new twist to the saga of—and I quote—'Captain Courageous and Crew?'"

"Please tell me you're kidding. She didn't." Another audible groan. "*Did* she?" Laurel squeaked.

"She did."

"Un. Believable." Laurel was outraged at the very thought of the reporter behaving so unethically.

"But get this," Cami continued. "She's not reporting the story we expected. This one might even be worse."

Laurel muttered darkly, "I find that hard to believe."

"Oh? Apparently, she and Dr. Fisk's secretary—sorry, administrative assistant—had quite the chat. Sourface Sally filled her in on all kinds of gossip and family dynamics. Catrina calls them 'confidential sources close to the couple,' but we all saw the two of them chatting it up in the hallway."

"What sort of gossip did Rita share? Again, do I even want to know?"

"Again, no. But I'll tell you, anyway. According to the report, our highly esteemed assistant chief had an affair a few years ago, and it almost cost her marriage, as well as her career. She was forced to step down from a very promising career in Chicago, which also upset her *husband's* career. She took a lesser position in Little Rock, but their daughter refused to leave. There's even some speculation that the daughter may not be the doctor's biological child, given her dark coloring and few Caucasian characteristics. There's speculation she may be a love child between Corinda, already a police officer with Chicago PD at the time, and a known leader of a black drug cartel there in the Windy City."

"Wow," Laurel murmured. "That was quite a

conversation for less than fifteen minutes!"

"*That's* what impresses you most about this story?" Cami demanded.

"No, but that's the only thing I can wrap my head around at the moment. I'm still processing the rest."

"Given these new revelations, I'm starting to rethink the pizza angle," Cami admitted.

"The pizza angle?"

"*Was* that pizza sauce on her shirt that night? Or was it blood?"

"I—I'm not sure," Laurel admitted.

Cami blew out a sigh of relief. "I'm glad to know I'm not the only one. Even before I heard these newest tidbits, it felt like something just wasn't right with those two."

"I agree completely. But Cade hasn't been very receptive to my input. I hope I'll have better luck this evening." Remembering their potential dinner plans, Laurel dropped the mostly uneaten sandwich. Not her favorite lunch to begin with, but all she had time to make this morning.

Cami picked up on the last of her statement. "This evening? As in, a date?" Her voice took on a teasing lilt.

"I hope not."

"What?" Her friend sounded shocked, not to mention disappointed. "Since when? I thought you two were working your way into becoming an item."

"We are. Maybe." She sounded uncertain, even to her own ears. "I think we are, anyway. But that's not what tonight is. Tonight is two busy people who have to eat and who can exchange information while doing so."

"Aw, you make it sound so romantic."

"You should see Danni's face." In spite of herself, Laurel laughed at the two drama queens she called her best friends. If Cami's expression matched Danni's, they both looked aghast. "She looks like I just admitted to knocking over a candy store."

"Same thing!" Danni called out, her voice loud enough to carry through to their friend. "Detective Hot Stuff is definitely eye candy, and she's making it a work date!"

Laurel wrinkled her nose at the accusation. "Enough, you two. At least one of us has to get back to work." With that, Laurel ended the call and stood.

"Since you're showing a lack of good judgment," Danni cautioned, "you're *definitely* coming with me to The Chicken Saturday night. No excuses."

Before returning to the desk, Laurel took a moment to shoot Cade a text.

I'll probably grab a bite to eat after work. Meet me there?

A few minutes later, bubbles danced across her screen.

Our usual?

Her smile was oddly sad. What did it say about their 'relationship' if the only place they had eaten together was at a fast-food Mexican restaurant? True, they had their own favorite table at *Mama G's Taqueria*, but a couple of shared meals didn't make it date worthy. She answered a patient's call button before responding.

Sure. I'll text you when I get off.

He was waiting for her outside the restaurant when she arrived. For a moment, she wished she wore something other than her scrubs, but she quickly reminded herself this wasn't a date. Like she told her friends, it was an exchange of information over a shared meal.

But when Cade put his hand on her waist and ushered her inside, it certainly *felt* like a date. Especially when he insisted on paying.

'Their' table by the window was free, so they gravitated to it without question, sliding into the booth seats opposite one another. Side by side was nice, but so was face to face, particularly with a face as handsome as Cade's.

"This is the first time I've been here since it's changed hands," Cade said. "You?"

"First time for me, too," she admitted. As silly as it seemed, she hadn't felt right about coming here without him.

Recently, one of the owners had been killed in a hit and run accident that turned out to be no accident at all, and the other faced time in prison on a multitude of charges. Some of the staff and long-time manager Delores Mendoza had pitched in to buy the original downtown Bryan location and keep it running, even though the other two locations were forced to close.

"I have a confession to make," Cade said, leaning across the table to speak in a conspiratorial tone. "I heard they were running a GoFundMe page to raise money to salvage the cafe." His brown eyes twinkled with a secret. "I made a contribution."

Laurel leaned in and made her own confession in a loud whisper. "So did I."

Cade captured her hand across the scarred vinyl four top. It felt intimate when his fingers entwined with hers.

"As much as I like the idea of us both having a stake in this place," he told her, "when I do take you on that much-anticipated date, I promise it will be some place that has linen tablecloths and true waiters."

"I don't care about fancy," Laurel replied, biting back the urge to add that she only cared about being with him.

"No, but you deserve it."

They shared a silly smile, which was interrupted when the server brought their meal to the table. "21?" he confirmed, exchanging the loaded tray for the numbered flag.

"That's us."

Sorting the order and settling the shared queso and chips between them, they dug into their meal with gusto. They kept the conversation to safe topics as they ate, but when Cade went back to order *sopapillas* and *churros*, Laurel sensed that was about to change. He slid into the seat beside her, daring her to kill the easy vibe they had going.

Drizzling a sugar-dusted *sopapilla* with honey, he offered Laurel the first bite. His dark gaze followed the tip of her tongue as she licked the powdered sugar from her lips.

"So good," she murmured, pretending not to notice the hunger in his eyes.

"I intend to find out." His mumbled reply was cryptic, but the look in his eyes left her heart thumping out a noisy beat. His gaze never left her lips as he lifted the puffy dough to his own mouth and bit slowly into it.

A nervous giggle bubbled up in her chest. They were in a crowded fast-food restaurant, seated behind a family with three rambunctious kids, and yet he made chewing seem so sensual. She struggled to control her swirling emotions.

"You're making a mess," Laurel admonished softly, reaching up to brush the residue from his cheek.

She saw a wicked thought come—and go—from his dark gaze. One of the children in the booth behind them bumped against the seat, jarring them both to their senses. A brief look of irritation flashed across his face, followed by a glimpse of regret. Both were quickly replaced with a devilish smile.

"Are you saying I can't be trusted to go to a fancy restaurant?"

Thankful to lighten the mood, Laurel pretended to ponder the question. "I have my doubts."

"We'll see about that." With a playful look of revenge, he stuffed the bulk of a *churro* into her mouth.

"How—How wude!" she sputtered around a delicious mouthful of cinnamon and crispy dough.

They savored the sweet treats and the light mood before Cade eventually spoiled the moment.

At least it's him this time, and not me, Laurel reasoned to herself.

Cade propped his elbows on the table and turned to look her in the eye. "FYI. You don't have to identify yourself when you call. By now, I know the sound of your voice. I hear it often enough in my dreams." He touched a black curl and watched it wrap itself around his finger. "But what, pray tell, was *possibly* important enough to *maybe* be urgent?"

He wasn't exactly making fun of her indecisive messages, so Laurel took no offense. Not after that dream comment, at any rate.

"We're having such a nice evening," she protested. "Are you sure you want to go there?"

His sigh was heavy as he dropped the curl and returned both arms to the table. "I suppose you've been translating again?"

"If only it were that easy."

She told him that his boss had come into the ER, glossing over the confidential details of her visit. "Suffice it to say, she's in no immediate danger," she assured him. "But she made several comments that I found… odd."

"Odd, how?" His tone was cautious.

Laurel squinched an eye and blurted out, "Like self-incriminating odd." She waited for the aftermath of her statement.

She felt Cade stiffen beside her, but he held his temper. She thought she heard him counting to ten.

"I'm not sure why you have this vendetta against ACAF—" he began.

"I don't!" Laurel broke in. "I don't have anything against her. My heart goes out to her and her loss. But... I know what I heard. Both times."

"Tell me what you *thought* you heard yesterday."

Hearing the inflection in his voice and understanding the inference, she snapped, "I know exactly what I heard. I just don't know what it meant."

She went through the conversation with him, reiterating key points. "She said it was her fault. That it wasn't supposed to happen. That she found him with the shoe."

"I understand all that. What I don't understand," he said coolly, "is how you took that as an admission of guilt."

"What was her fault, if not his death? Maybe she found him with another woman's shoes and confronted him with it. In a fit of anger, maybe she struck out at him. It wasn't supposed to kill him, but it did. Maybe *that* was her confession."

"Or maybe," he countered, "she blames herself for moving here and bringing him to the town where he ultimately died. Maybe she meant his sudden death wasn't part of their plans for a happily ever after, and this wasn't supposed to happen to them. Maybe when she found him, the shoe was already wedged into his chest."

In all fairness, Laurel admitted, "That's what she claimed, but that doesn't mean it's true."

"It doesn't mean it's not true, either."

Laurel dared changing the subject. "Did you hear the breaking news report today?"

"Nah," he said with heavy sarcasm. "I missed hearing my boss' name dragged through the mud on several major and all local networks, as well as on social media in every size, shape, and form."

"You don't have to be nasty about it," Laurel huffed.

Cade blew out a weary breath. "I'm sorry, Laurel," he apologized. "I don't mean to take my frustrations out on you. I just wish I knew who this 'confidential source close to the couple' was."

"I can help you there," she said brightly. "I know exactly who it was. Or, at least, I have a very good idea." She told him about Rita Bernard accompanying his boss to the hospital and later seeing her speaking with the reporter in conspiratorial tones.

"Plus," she added, "I noticed she had a rather large foot for a woman."

"What are you saying, Nancy?" he all but growled.

"I'm saying the fuzzy slippers could have belonged to her. I'm saying I sensed tension between the two women, and no real camaraderie. I think it's possible Dr. Fisk was having an affair with Rita Bernard, his wife caught him with the slippers and knew he was cheating on her, and confronted him with the fact. Things could have easily escalated from there."

"Nothing but speculation," Cade ground out. He glanced around, as if suddenly realizing they were having this conversation in a very public place. Luckily, no one seemed to be paying them much attention. "Are you ready?"

Laurel gave a jerky nod of her head and slid from the booth behind him. Their earlier ease having dissolved like powdered sugar on hot dough, their movements were now stiff as they walked from the restaurant and toward her car.

"Laurel," he began. His tone was tentative.

She put up a hand to stop him. "No. I know you don't believe me, but isn't there a chance you're too close to this case to look at it objectively?"

"You don't understand."

"Yes, I think that I do. I get that she's your boss. I know it puts you in a difficult position. And I know that I'm just your… whatever it is I am to you. Probably just some pesky nurse who you think is playing Nancy Drew again—"

"You're so much more to me than that, Laurel," he broke in as they stopped beside her car. "And you know it!" He turned to her with a challenge in his dark eyes, daring her to dispute his claim.

"Whatever," she said, brushing his claim away like a gnat on the breeze.

"Don't say whatever!" he said almost angrily. He took her arm, his grip firm but gentle. "You know there's something between us."

"I certainly do," she quipped bitterly. "Our careers. And, apparently, your boss!"

"So... what? I'm supposed to choose between the two of you?"

"Of course not! You're supposed to do your job and see that justice is served!"

He flinched, absorbing the words she flung at him like a physical blow.

Laurel grabbed for his arm, trying uselessly to pull back her thoughtless words. "I—I didn't mean that."

"Yes. You did." His voice didn't sound angry. It sounded sad and just a bit resigned.

"But I didn't mean it the way it came out. I meant..."

"I know what you meant, Laurel." His voice was low. "And you're right."

Her head jerked up in surprise, but his gaze was averted as he stared off into the distance. "Maybe I am too close to this case. Maybe I'm not being objective."

She slid her hand along the hard-as-steel column of his arm, rubbing it to infuse a sense of warmth into her words. Around them, the chilled night air hovered close. "I know you're in an impossible position. But I also know you're a fair and just man. Maddening at times," she said with a smile, "but you're dedicated to the law and to bringing justice to the victims who can't speak for themselves. You'll find a way to be loyal to your boss, while still being loyal to your oath."

A small smile crooked the corner of his mouth.

"You're putting a lot of faith in me. I'm not sure I deserve it."

"Yes. I am." Her words were slow and distinct. "And yes. You do."

He opened his arms, and she stepped into his embrace. They simply held each other in the coolness of the night, ignoring the cars and the people around them. For the moment, they were cocooned in their own little world of warmth and encouragement.

After a long moment, Cade spoke, "I'll see you home."

"That's not necessary."

"I won't come in. I just want to know you make it home safely."

Laurel reached up to brush a kiss across his cheek, still slightly sticky from the honey and sugar. "You're a good man, Cade Resnick. I know you'll do the right thing."

"If I were a genuinely good man," he said, his voice thick with objection, and something more, "I'd be able to resist doing this." He fisted a handful of her hair and drew her close, lowering his face to hers.

It wasn't where he had intended for their first kiss to take place, and yet it was oddly perfect. It was just outside *their* restaurant, with *their* table visible through the window. The harsh glare of the overhead security light gave the night an unnatural glow, nothing like the starlit sky he had envisioned. But when she had wrapped her unique scent around him and whispered her faith in him, he couldn't resist. Kissing her became as elemental to him as breathing.

Laurel didn't care that a group of teenagers snickered as they passed by, with calls of 'get a room' and 'talk about intensive care!' She didn't notice when the family of five crossed behind them and the kids oohed and ahhed, one of them asking their mother why grownups liked to kiss on the lips and not the cheek. She didn't care that she wore scrubs and sensible shoes, and that her makeup was long gone for the day. She didn't care that they both tasted of onions and garlic. All she tasted was Cade and the sweet remnants of honey and cinnamon.

They pulled away slowly, reluctant to end the imperfectly perfect moment. The magical first kiss left them both hungry for more, but they were in a public parking lot, and the kiss hadn't solved any of their problems. In many ways, it only complicated things further.

Laurel refused to dwell on the negative. With an impish smile, she said, "Now that we've cleared *that* hurdle"—she brushed a finger across his lips and tossed her hair smartly— "you can see about making those dinner reservations."

He caught her to him for one more hard, fast kiss. "Done," he promised, releasing her with a laugh. "I'll follow you home. Blink your porch lights when you're safely inside."

"Aye, aye, captain," she saluted as she slid into her seat.

Belatedly, she realized her words may have reminded him of his own captain—or, more precisely, his assistant chief—and the duty before him.

Once again, she had probably killed the moment.

But oh, she thought dreamily, as she put her seatbelt on and pulled out of the driveway, *what a moment!*

CHAPTER NINE

First thing the next morning, Cade brought in new whiteboards and mapped out the evidence using different identification tags. Instead of using names, he used the generic titles of 'victim' and 'wife,' and a numbering system for 'witnesses' and 'suspects.'

The witnesses were few, the suspects zero. Leaving off names gave the board the impersonal, professional touch it needed but did little to make the picture any clearer.

Over at *Texas General*, Laurel's day was going smoother than expected. It had been a relatively quiet morning, and they were adequately staffed, so when her superior needed something delivered to a doctor's office across town, Laurel volunteered. Her co-workers talked her into making a *Layne's Chicken Fingers* run on the way back.

Laurel's tummy growled as she crawled from her car with the aromatic bags. At her superior's request, she carried a box of mixed pastries in the other hand. If she had a third hand, she would have brought coffee, as well, but the break room's brew would have to suffice.

Busy thinking about the expertly blended dipping sauce for the chicken fingers, she paid little attention to her surroundings. She had tried duplicating the recipe at home, but she still didn't have it quite right. Something was missing, but what? She sifted through the flavors in her mind, not noticing where she walked. She didn't even see the news van until she was upon it.

"Nurse? Nurse!" a voice called. "Can I have a word with you for a moment?"

Laurel jerked her head up in surprise, alarmed to see that she had walked directly into the path of the camera crew. She vehemently shook her head, even before she noticed the woman behind the mic.

Catrina Carter.

"Ah, we meet again," Catrina all but smirked. She dropped her mic, correctly assuming Laurel had no intention of speaking with her.

"Hello, Ms. Carter," Laurel said with cool professionalism. She kept steadily on track toward the sliding glass doors.

Catrina eyed the food in her hands. "My, aren't we hungry today." Not taking the hint, Catrina tagged alongside her.

"Even over-worked nurses have to eat."

With her gaze trained straight ahead, Laurel missed the merriment dancing in the reporter's eyes. "And not very healthily, from the looks of it," Catrina admonished.

"I take it you're feeling better since your visit to the ER?"

"Absolutely. Visiting your ER provided me with just the pick me up I needed. I found it very educational. And I met such interesting people there!"

Sarcasm dripped from Laurel's voice. "So I heard."

"I've been told that medicine isn't always an exact science," Catrina went on in an artificially bright voice, "and often comes down to having the right information at the right time. I couldn't agree more. I learned *so much* while visiting your little emergency room." She was taunting Laurel, clearly referring to her visit with Rita Bernard.

"Again, Ms. Carter, I can't stress the importance of confidentiality and ethical conduct enough."

"I *completely* agree!" Hearing the other woman's gushing response, Laurel realized she had stepped right into that one. From the corner of her eye, she saw Catrina nod with an exaggerated look of concern. "Do you think it's ethical for a member of law enforcement to have an extramarital affair with a known criminal? Or with anyone, for that matter, if he or she is married?"

"I'm a registered nurse, Ms. Carter. My expertise lies in the medical field, not in law enforcement or ethics."

"Are you saying you don't practice ethics?"

"Of course I do!" Laurel shot an indignant look at the reporter, before returning her gaze to the path ahead. Under her breath, she pointedly added, "Unlike some people in this conversation."

"I have it on good authority that the assistant chief of police of the College Station Police Department and her husband, the recently murdered Dr. Arnold Fisk, have a history of infidelity in their marriage. Do you find that as suspicious as I do?"

"I find it of no consequence, actually." Laurel glanced down at the mic in the other woman's hand, confirming that their conversation wasn't being recorded. Otherwise, she wouldn't have spoken a word beyond hello.

"Really? You don't think that could be motive for murder?"

"I hardly see how. It's much easier to get a divorce than it is to murder someone."

The hike to the entrance had never felt so long. The

staff was encouraged to park at the rear of the parking lot, leaving the closer spaces for patients and guests. Laurel usually looked for a spot at the very back, thinking of it as good exercise. Right now, she regretted the yards of asphalt still stretching between her and the safety of the door. The press still wasn't allowed inside the hospital unless they sneaked in like "Tina" had done.

"What if the good doctor was the one having the affair?" the reporter suggested smugly.

Laurel ignored the question and kept walking.

She had a terrible poker face. Catrina Carter noticed the brief look of uncertainty that crossed her face and focused on it with laser-like intensity.

"He was, wasn't he?" Catrina pressed.

"I have no idea whether or not the doctor was having an affair. And it's none of my concern. This conversation is over."

"That's it!" the reporter correctly guessed. Her voice filled with almost glee-like enthusiasm, her steps faltering with the revelation. She scrambled to keep up with the nurse's brisk pace, her accusations coming hard and fast. "You think the doctor was cheating on his wife! You think the doctor was having an affair and that his wife killed him because of it! You were the attending nurse when he came in. Did he say something to make you draw this conclusion?"

Laurel stared stonily ahead.

"I understand the doctor spent a great deal of time at his office and at his 'man-cave' in the backyard of the couple's home. Is that where you think this alleged affair took place?"

Laurel kept walking, her steps quickening.

"No one will confirm where the murder took place, but the ambulance was dispatched to their home address in an exclusive gated community. There's speculation he was found in his man-cave out back. Do you think this was his own private love shack? Did he give any indication of knowing who had stabbed him? Did he ask for his wife? Did he call anyone's name while he was in your care?"

Almost to the door...

"Nurse Benson, don't you want to see justice serviced? Didn't you take an oath to protect your patients? If you have a clue as to who harmed your patient and caused his subsequent death, don't you owe it to Dr. Fisk—and to all the patients in your care—to come forward with this evidence?"

Laurel turned and made a brisk comment to the pesky reporter.

"I've been in contact with the College Station Police Department and given my statement on the condition of the patient when he arrived. That is the full scope of my knowledge and involvement in the case. I have nothing further to contribute."

She turned her back on the other woman and stood trembling outside the glass doors, wondering if it were safe to swipe her ID card to gain entrance. Would the pushy woman storm her way inside? Would she somehow steal and duplicate the access code?

Before she decided on how to proceed, the security officer stationed just inside the doors spotted the nurse and granted access to the door. Laurel slipped inside while he asked the reporter to step back, citing the fifty-foot no-press zone. Before scurrying down the hall, Laurel glanced over her shoulder to make certain Catrina complied.

Only then did she notice the cameraman directly behind her.

A CASE OF DEATH IN DISGUISE

With a sinking feeling in the pit of her stomach, Laurel realized he had been there the entire time.

Laurel was late getting home that evening. Her phone rang as she kicked her shoes off and locked the door behind her.

Cade's number flashed across her screen, but her pleased smile died a sudden death when she heard his thunderous tone.

"What. Did. You. Do."

Just a hunch, but the handsome detective was highly irate. Having no idea what she supposedly did to deserve such a cold reception, her reply was flippant, "What did I do about what?"

"Have you seen the news?"

"I literally just walked through the door. I've been at work all day. After a relatively quiet morning, the afternoon was complete chaos. Two wrecks, a locker-room fight that required stitches for three teenagers—girls, no less—and one coach, a heart patient we had to fly to *St. Luke's* in Houston, and a man who tried to cut his thumb off with a pocketknife. No time for TV."

"Apparently you had time for *Layne's*." It sounded like an accusation.

"I fail to see... Wait. How do you even *know* that?"

"I recognized the bag you were holding."

"If you were at the hospital, why didn't you stop by and say hello?"

"I wasn't at the hospital, Laurel." His voice was tight with impatience and what still sounded like accusation.

Laurel put a hand to her pounding head and sank onto the sofa. "Look, I have a headache. Please stop talking in riddles and tell me what you think I did. And while you're at it, explain how you know what I had for lunch. Are you spying on me?"

His short burst of laughter lacked anything resembling humor. "Why would I need to spy, when it's right there on television for the whole world to see?"

"I have no idea what you're talking about. I'm tired, I'm hungry, and my head is killing me. Your yelling doesn't help. What are you talking about?"

"You talked to that reporter!"

After a crazy afternoon, Laurel had actually forgotten about the encounter with Catrina and the cameraman who had stealthily followed them.

"Not by choice." She squirmed with a sudden sense of unease. "And just briefly."

"Long enough to sell out me and the entire College Station Police Department!"

"What—What are you talking about? I didn't tell her anything."

"You accused my boss of murder!" Cade bellowed.

"I did no such thing!"

"Watch the interview. It's all over the internet and the news apps. Watch it, and then call me a liar."

With those sharply spoken words, Cade hung up.

Laurel was more baffled than she was angry. That would come later. She pulled the local news app up on her phone and groaned. That was her face, all right, frozen unattractively in mid-sentence.

Am I really that short? And speaking of sour face. I look like I sucked one of Rita Bernard's lemons.

She played the interview, but it didn't make sense. That wasn't what she had said. She played it for the third time before realization sank in.

"That witch! She edited the tape! She purposely

distorted my words!"

Laurel played the piece again, her chin hanging almost to her knees. Even on this fourth viewing, she couldn't help but gasp in disbelief.

"We're live in College Station, Texas speaking with Laurel Benson, who works here in *Texas General Hospital's* ER," Catrina said into a microphone emblazoned with the WXYZ logo. After showcasing the hospital behind her, she turned on an angle to continue, "I understand you were the attending nurse when Dr. Arnold Fisk, CEO of the *Brazos Valley Methodist Hospital* was brought in by ambulance *here* on Saturday evening. Can you tell me what, exactly, it is that you do here?" She tilted the mic away from herself before the camera panned to Laurel's face.

It was a side shot, but Laurel's voice came through clearly. "I'm a registered nurse."

"I've been told that medicine isn't always an exact science and often comes down to having the right information at the right time. I couldn't agree more. I learned *so much* while visiting your little emergency room, and I appreciate your willingness to speak with me so candidly this afternoon. Does the gag order issued by your employer concern you at all?"

"I find it of no consequence, actually." The camera showed Laurel staring stonily ahead. "Even over-worked nurses have to eat."

"Absolutely. Now, if I understand it, the police have spoken with you about Dr. Fisk's condition when he arrived in the emergency room, correct?"

"I've been in contact with the College Station Police Department and given my statement."

"Confidential sources tell me you may have heard the doctor name his attacker that night."

"I heard."

"When you reported this to the police, do you feel your eyewitness testimony was handled in a professional manner?"

"My expertise lies in the medical field, not in law enforcement. I can't stress the importance of ethical conduct enough... Unlike some people in the police department."

"Interesting," Catrina hummed into the microphone, pushing her hair back as the breeze tossed it into her face. "It's a well-known fact that the assistant chief of police with the College Station Police Department is the wife of the recently murdered Dr. Arnold Fisk. Many people, yourself included from what I understand, feel this is a conflict of interest for Assistant Chief Addison-Fisk, given that her detectives are in charge of the investigation. Most say it's also an ethical matter. Do you agree?"

"Again, my expertise lies in the medical field, not ethics."

"I have it on good authority that the couple has a history of infidelity in their marriage."

"The doctor was having an affair."

"And you think that could be motive for murder?" The reporter looked appropriately shocked but recovered quickly. "You think the doctor was having an affair and that his wife killed him because of it!"

"Of course I do!"

Catrina turned back to the camera with a wide smile. "And there you have it, folks. Attending nurse and eyewitness Laurel Benson with *Texas General* who claims Assistant Chief Addison-Fisk is responsible for her husband's murder. Stay tuned to WXYZ. We'll have much more on this breaking story at ten."

Trembling with anger, Laurel stumbled toward the door when the banging began. She wasn't at all surprised to see Cade's face through the peephole. He still looked furious.

It was the same way she felt. When she opened the door, he barged inside, but she spoke before he could. "It was a setup, Cade. You have to believe me."

"You had no business talking to her in the first place!"

"I realize that. But, believe me, she completely misconstrued the conversation and edited it so that what you saw on the replay was nothing close to what was said in reality."

"Can you prove that?" he challenged.

"I think so. Let me get my computer, and I'll show you."

Her phone rang as she left the angry detective in her living room to grab her laptop. It was the first call of many, most of which she ignored. When she saw the hospital number pop up, she answered immediately.

Cade paced the floor while she was on the phone. He could only hear her side of the call, and it wasn't pleasant.

"Yes, I saw it," she told the person on the other end. "I want you to know the conversation was edited and pieced together. I didn't grant an interview. The reporter followed me in the parking lot and turned innocent remarks into something completely false.... Yes, you're right, of course. I should have never spoken to her. In all fairness, however, she had her mic down to her side, and I never saw the cameraman... A detective is here with me now, and we're about to go over the tape. I'm showing him how I know the tape is fake, and he'll advise me on how to proceed... Thank you. First thing tomorrow morning."

Her expression was grim as she hung up the phone. It went without saying that she was in trouble and could possibly lose her job over the unsanctioned interview. He felt a stab of regret for adding to her distress. Had he been too hasty in thinking the worst of her? Maybe she had been set up by a manipulative reporter. It wouldn't be the first time.

"You're going to wear out the hardwood," Laurel snapped. "Come sit by me, and I'll prove my innocence."

"Laurel..."

Her tone was testy. "Just sit."

Amused by the feisty attitude of the spitfire issuing orders, he did as told.

"Here. First thing. She's holding the mic and introducing herself," Laurel pointed out as she paused the video. "She's standing in a different spot than she is here. You can tell by the angle of the building." The video began to play again. "See? And see how she appears to hold the microphone out toward me, yet it's not in any of the shots of me? That's because I made certain her mic was down before I even said hello. I just assumed it was also off. That's on me." She was big enough to own her mistake.

Laurel moved the laptop to sit upon both their knees, allowing him a clearer view. "I'm not looking into the camera in a single shot. If I granted the interview, as she claimed I did, I would look the camera, or her, in the eye. Don't you find that the least bit odd?"

"I suppose."

She sniffed at his lukewarm reply. "I made the remark about nurses having to eat at the very beginning, when she made some snide comment about how much food I was carrying. She makes it sound as if I took money for talking to her, which I would think was unethical and could possibly be considered extortion on her part. Anyway... my comment about speaking with the police was the very last thing I said, when I told her I had nothing more to contribute."

"How did she know Fisk spoke that night? And that you 'interpreted' his mumbo jumbo?" He used air quotes around the word interpreted.

"I think it was a lucky guess. My comment about hearing something was in reference to her 'informative' trip to the ER and all the interesting people she met. Again, edited and out of context."

Laurel hit play again, stopping it a few seconds later. "What I said here was 'unlike some people in this conversation.' She edited it to say, 'Police Department.' If you notice, you saw this same car—" she indicated a green sedan turning the corner in the background— "in the same place when I said the same words, 'Police Department,' in reference to giving a statement."

Impressed, Cade looked at her with appreciation. He had missed that the first fifty times he watched the video.

"Eyes back on the screen," she said sharply. "See how the wind blows her hair into her face? Did you see a single hair out of place in any other part of the video? No. That's because it wasn't at all windy when I left. I didn't even bother with a sweater."

"Laurel, I—"

She sensed his impending apology. She was in no mood to hear it. She went on with her analysis.

"I never said that about a conflict of interest for the police department. And this part? She cut out the first of the sentence, when I said 'whether or not' the doctor was having an affair. If that were a statement in itself, I would have used a different inflection. *She's* the one who made the claim. And that's when I responded that it was none of my concern."

Still not completely convinced of her innocence, he pointed out an indisputable truth. "But she said you believed the doctor was having an affair and that you thought his wife had killed him. And you do, don't you?"

"Honestly? Yes." Cade sucked in a sharp breath at her confession. "But I swear, I never told her that. She made a lucky guess, and I have a terrible poker face."

"But what you said... 'Of course I do!'"

"Was in response to some snide remark about me not practicing ethical behavior." Laurel jabbed her finger back toward the screen. "And if none of that convinces you, look at the position of the sun in the sky. Her opening and closing remarks were clearly taken some time after I made my side-view comments."

Snapping her computer shut and barely missing his fingers resting there, Laurel abruptly stood and marched to the window to stare blindly through the pulled shutters.

"If what you say is true—" Cade began.

Laurel whirled on him, her hazel eyes shooting out flames. "*IF?*" she shrieked.

He showed his palms in surrender as he, too, stood. "I think you have a defamation lawsuit on your hands. You can sue her and the television station for making false statements and intent to commit fraud."

Suddenly weary, Laurel sagged against the wall. "I'll let the hospital lawyers tackle that." She pushed a hand through her tumbled curls. "Assuming I still have a job come tomorrow morning. Our hospital administrator wants to meet with me first thing."

"I will personally call and back you up," Cade told her, moving closer to her. His brown eyes warmed with sincerity. "I do believe you, Laurel. That tape was edited and intended to misstate the facts."

When he would have reached for her, Laurel moved away. She made her way to the door.

"I think you should go."

"Laurel," he pleaded.

"Please leave."

"I'm sorry, Laurel. I jumped to conclusions. I should have given you the benefit of the doubt."

"People are always so eager to believe anything they see on the news or on the internet. I thought you, of all people, knew better."

Cade hung his head in shame. "You're right. I should have. All I can say is that I'm sorry."

Now the anger set in. She jabbed a finger into his chest. "And how *dare* you hang up on me!"

He tried hard not to smile. He knew she had every right to be angry. He knew he was at fault. He knew how serious the entire situation was, particularly concerning her job. Even his own job could be in jeopardy, if ACAF blamed him for this mess.

But most of all, Cade knew that before him stood the most beautiful and exciting woman he had been with in a very long time. Despite the solemnness of the occasion, his heart had taken flight.

"Don't you laugh at me!" she hissed, enraged by the tiny smile hovering on his lips.

"I'm not. I swear, I'm not laughing at you."

Laurel jerked the door open and flung her arm toward

the porch. "Get out. Just... get out."

He stopped just long enough to brush a kiss across her lips. She growled in protest, which made his smile burst free.

"Just so you know," he said, hurrying over the threshold, "you're incredibly beautiful when you're angry. And I really am very sorry for doubting you."

Incensed, Laurel grabbed the first thing she could find. She shrieked again in anger, hurling the hapless cornucopia at his hastily retreating back. "Leave! Go! Away!"

The sound of his laughter trailed in the night air as Laurel slammed the door hard enough to rattle the windows.

CHAPTER TEN

As promised, Laurel reported to the administrator's office the moment she arrived at work. It didn't escape her notice that it was Saturday, and that administration normally had the weekend off. Seeing a room full of her higher ups and hospital lawyers spoke to how serious the situation was and made her immensely nervous.

She took a deep breath of courage and stepped into the lion's den.

Also as promised, Cade had already spoken to the head of administration on her behalf. After going through the same process with administrators as she had with the detective, she felt confident she proved her claims of an edited tape. Promising to handle all legal matters on her behalf, the bosses allowed her to return to work and bid her a pleasant day.

Like that's going to happen, Laurel sulked, heading back to the ER. At least they believed me and are on my side. Now to convince the rest of the world...

"All the more reason for you to join us tonight at The Chicken," Danni insisted.

"Honestly, I don't think I'd be any fun. No need for me to drag you down."

"So let us lift you up," Danni said, putting an arm around her shoulders and giving them a squeeze.

"But..."

"But nothing. You need this."

Maybe she did, Laurel acknowledged. She rarely did anything with her friends these days. She didn't mean to neglect their friendship, but between work, continuing education classes, and those never-ending projects around the house—a small enough price to pay for living in the charming old craftsman—she admitted to being stingy with her free time. Most free evenings found her curled up in her reading nook in the living room or, when weather allowed, on her front porch swing, spending a quiet night at home to recharge.

While going to a college bar wasn't her idea of fun, hearing live music and being with friends was. She didn't relish sitting home alone tonight, and for once, even the thought of a long, soaking bath sounded more boring than relaxing.

Her mind strayed to a certain detective, but she reminded herself that she wasn't speaking to him. He had called or texted a dozen times since the cornucopia incident, but she wasn't ready to talk to him. Her heart still smarted from his initial distrust. If he thought she was so unscrupulous and so lacking in integrity, perhaps he wasn't the man she thought he was. Certainly not the man for her.

Yes, going out with friends tonight would be good for her. And it might just offer the distraction she needed.

"See? Aren't you glad you came with us tonight?" Cami asked, linking her arm through Laurel's as the three friends pushed their way out the doors of the overflowing bar.

"And look!" Danni beamed, pointing to her watch. "It's not even midnight. Just as I promised."

"Yes, you did." Laurel smiled at her friend with the rusty corkscrew curls. She turned to smile at the one on the other side, the one sporting blonde curls. "And yes, I am."

"The Curly Girls, back in action!" Danni proclaimed.

Laurel tipped back her head and laughed, sending her own dark curls dancing. Few people believed that their hairstyles and colors were natural, even though they were. "I'm glad I came with you this evening," she admitted. "That was fun."

"We don't have to go home yet. We could hit another bar. Northgate is hopping tonight," Cami said, looking around the epicenter of nightlife in the bustling college town.

"True. But I'm not. You know I turn into a pumpkin after midnight."

"Don't you dare repeat this to a soul," Danni said, dipping her head so that her friends had to do the same to hear her words, "but I think I'm getting too old for this. It's just not the same as it was when I first moved here."

"That was... what? Five years ago?" Laurel asked. She had been back for three.

"Yep. Five years of getting up at the crack of dawn and walking my feet to the bone has taken its toll."

"I hear you," Cami agreed. "That was one of the main reasons Randy and I broke up. He was still into bar hopping when I was more into popcorn and movies at home."

"It's fine to do this occasionally." Laurel played devil's advocate as they shuffled along the sidewalk. Her smile turned mischievous. "I'm willing to try it again in a year or so."

They all laughed as they made their way toward the parking lots out back. It was difficult muddling through the crowded space with their arms linked, so they resorted to single file in the thickest of foot traffic.

"I certainly don't miss *this*!" Laurel muttered, as a woman jostled into her. The force almost knocked the petite nurse off her feet.

The woman came from a darkened doorway marked *Rainbow Bridge*. Her stance was unsteady, and she seemed to wobble for a moment on her high-heeled shoes. Of course, Laurel noted, she was a very tall woman to begin with, and walking in those things had to be difficult, especially when drinking. Something about her looked vaguely familiar, but Laurel didn't recognize the coiffed purple hair or the matching eye shadow. In fact, almost everything about the woman was purple, from her long, dangling earrings and filmy chiffon blouse, down to her short purple skirt and fishnet hose.

The person stared at Laurel for a long moment, as her obsidian eyes adjusted to the bright neon signs and the colorful lights strung along the different bars and businesses.

Eyes dilated. Nostrils slightly flared. Still a bit unsteady on her feet, Laurel assessed. Old habits die hard, even when she wasn't in a hospital setting. Probably had too much to drink, or too many recreational drugs. Maybe both. At any rate, moving along now…

She made a show of pulling away from the woman's proximity and scurrying to keep pace with her friends.

"What happened?" Danni wanted to know. "For a minute there, I thought we lost you."

"Some woman bumped into me, coming out of that

bar. She was about a foot taller than I am and almost knocked me over!"

"What bar?" Cami asked.

"*Rainbow* something." Laurel pointed behind them. "That woman all in purple."

"Uhm, I hate to tell you, but that isn't a woman," Danni said, her eyes dancing with laughter. "*Rainbow Bridge* is a gay bar."

Laurel looked back over her shoulder. She shook her head to get it straight. "Those drinks must have been stronger than I imagined," she admitted. She only had two and hadn't thought either of them were particularly potent.

"That was a man, all right." Cami laughed along with Danni. Then she added, "But he was in drag, so you're not as drunk as you think."

"Thank goodness!" Laurel slapped a hand to her chest. "I was getting worried there for a minute. If I can't handle a couple of mixed drinks, I'm aging faster than I thought!"

The friends linked arms again, laughing and moving along their way.

And when Cade's number popped up on her phone again, Laurel wasn't even tempted to take his call.

The next morning, Laurel's head pounded, and her stomach felt queasy. Maybe visiting that upscale wine bar hadn't been such a smart move, after all. It may have restored their sense of sophistication and style, but it hadn't done much for staying sober. Not that any of them had been drunk, exactly. Just a bit lightheaded by the time they left at one.

Lack of sleep fogged her mind and left her tummy unsettled. A gallon or two of coffee and some crackers should fix her right up. If Cade would stop blowing her phone up at this ungodly time of morning, she'd be good.

As she drove to work, she gave in, putting him on speakerphone. She answered with a sharp, "What?"

"It's about time you answered!" he growled. "I was about to put out a BOLO on you."

"Seriously?" She stared at her phone in disbelief.

"Seriously. I've been calling you since yesterday morning."

"I considered batting for a thousand, but I don't have time for that today," she said smartly.

"Where were you last night?" he demanded.

"Out."

"You told me you were working this weekend."

"I am. And I don't like that accusatory tone in your voice."

"Just to be clear. You couldn't go out with me, but you could go out with someone else?" She heard the sulk in his voice, which did little to cover the underlying hint of hurt. She felt a pang of guilt but chose to ignore it. She was in no mood to placate him. Not after he had doubted her the way he had.

"Yes. Danni, Cami, and I had a wonderful time. A friend was playing in Northgate, and we went to support him."

"Northgate? Seriously?" The disdain was obvious in his voice.

"Yes, Rip Van Winkle. Northgate. They offer a senior citizen discount if you arrive before ten."

"Very funny. I just didn't think that was your style." He sounded disappointed, which Laurel found oddly reassuring.

She couldn't hold in the sigh escaping her lips. "It's not. We ducked out early and wound up at *The Wine Depot*."

"Please tell me you didn't drink and drive."

He *was* law enforcement, but Laurel couldn't lie. "We coasted back to Danni's place. She only lives a couple of blocks from there. Her roommate drove Cami and me home. But we weren't drunk," she was quick to point out. "Just… happy." That was as good a word as any to describe their evening. It *had* been fun.

"Happy." He sounded dubious.

Becoming irritated with the way he repeated everything she said, she snapped, "Yes, happy. You have a problem with that?"

"I have a problem with you not answering my calls. I have a problem with you turning me down, then going bar-hopping with your friends."

"One kiss," she hissed. "It was. One. Kiss. We haven't even been out on an official date yet."

"And whose fault is that? I asked you for last night, remember?" he shot back at her.

"Here's an All-Points Bulletin, Officer Resnick," she said coolly. "You don't get to dictate what I do. If I want to go out with my best friends and get rip-roaring drunk—which I don't, but I could, if I wanted to—then it's none of your business. Got that?"

His vice was stiff and distant. "In. Spades." She swore she could feel his finger hovering over the 'end' button.

"Don't you dare hang up on me! If you do, I swear I'll never speak to you again!" she threatened.

"That may be a problem, Nurse Benson," he said in a stiff voice, "because the chief would like to speak to you. He asked me to drive you down to the station for a . . .

conversation." He paused over the word *conversation*, giving it weight.

"Am I under arrest?" she asked stiffly.

"Of course not."

"Then it will have to wait until tomorrow when I'm off. I have to go now. I'm pulling in at the hospital."

Okay, it was still a half-mile away, but he didn't have to know that.

Maybe she *could* lie, after all.

"You look terrible," Cami told her frankly. "Please tell me I don't look that bad, too."

"You look gorgeous, as usual," Laurel said with a mixture of truth and resentment.

"I know you didn't drink that much, so you can't have a hangover. Not unless you went home and emptied a bottle."

"I went home and crashed. I'm not hungover. Just worried. And Cade and I are fighting."

Eyebrows up, Cami said, "I didn't realize your relationship had progressed to the fighting phase."

"Are you kidding? That's where it started," Laurel answered on a grunt.

Amid flashing call lights and buzzing pagers, Cami said, "We'll continue this conversation at break. We'll get Danni on the line and have a three-way."

Alberto, one of their most lovable and geekiest techs, walked up in time to hear the end of her sentence. "Count me in!" He grinned.

"In your dreams, tech boy."

"I'm an X-ray technician," he reminded her. "You know I can literally see through your clothes."

"Cannot!" Cami argued. Just in case, she crossed her arms over her chest.

Laughing at their antics, Laurel padded down the hallway to Room 2. "At break," she confirmed.

It turned out to be lunch, and a late one, at that. Cami and Laurel managed to coordinate their breaks together, where they called Danni on Zoom.

"I know I don't have on makeup," the redhead began, "but surely I don't look as rough as you two!"

"Busy morning," Laurel sighed.

In a loud stage whisper, Cami added, "She and Cade are *fighting*."

Like their friend, Danni was surprised. "Fighting? I didn't know you were in the fighting phase of your relationship."

"What does that even mean?" Laurel asked irritably.

"Fighting doesn't usually happen until *after* the first make-out session."

Seeing the way Laurel avoided her gaze, Cami squealed. "Really? When? Why didn't you tell us?"

Laurel rolled her eyes. "What are we, thirteen? And it wasn't a make-out session. It was one kiss." *But man, what a kiss!*

"When?" Danni demanded.

She thought back. "A couple of nights ago?"

"Wait." Cami's voice came out in disbelief. "Wait, wait, wait, wait, wait. You're just now telling us?" She nudged her foot against Laurel's legs, almost knocking them from their perch on the nearby chair. "We spent the entire evening together last night, and you never thought to tell us?"

"It slipped my mind?"

"Try again." Danni's voice was droll.

"I blocked it from my mind?"

"Slightly more believable," Cami deduced, "but highly improbable."

"And how did that work out for you?" Danni wanted to know.

Laurel twisted her mouth. "I should have blocked him from my phone. He just about blew it up, calling every thirty minutes."

Danni leaned forward into the screen. "This sounds interesting."

"I never took him for the possessive type," Laurel confessed, "but he nearly blew a gasket when he found out I went out with you two, instead of him."

"You seriously chose us over him? Are you insane?" Danni demanded.

"We had that fight, remember?"

"Kinda hard to remember," Cami pointed out, "when we knew nothing about it." Her tone turned accusatory. "I can't believe you haven't already told us this."

"It had to do with that so-called interview. He thought I sold him out. He believes me now, but it's just the idea that he thought I was capable of something so devious and underhanded. Something so unethical." She shook her head in disappointment. "And now, his boss wants to talk to me, and I'm worried I might be in legal trouble."

"But I thought brass cleared you of any wrongdoing. They're sending in *Texas General* lawyers for you," Danni said with a confused frown.

"The hospital cleared me, but I'm not sure the police have. They may think I know something."

Cami looked conflicted. "You kinda sorta do," she pointed out.

"What are you two talking about?" Danni wanted to know. "What haven't you told me?"

"Nothing I plan on telling you here," Laurel hissed, looking around the empty room. Luckily, there was no one else in the break room but them.

"Fine," Danni agreed. "Call me tonight." She flashed a dimpled smile across the screen. "You can give me the juicy details of the kiss then, too."

"Not without me, she can't!" Cami protested.

"Again," Laurel reminded her friends, rolling her eyes like the teenager she denied being, "we're not thirteen."

"Forget the phone call," Danni decided. "Tacos at my house when you get off work."

"Not in front of Annabelle," Laurel said uncomfortably. The fewer who knew of the doctor's confession, the better. "Bring them to my house, instead. Oh, and Curly Girls? No margaritas tonight. I need a clear head when I go to the police station tomorrow."

CHAPTER ELEVEN

Cade offered to drive her to the station, but Laurel chose to bring her own car. The handsome detective met her out front and ushered her inside with cool professionalism.

"Chief of Police Alex Moore," the burly lawman greeted her across a massive oak desk. "It's a pleasure to meet you, Miss Benson. Please, have a seat."

With formalities and small talk out of the way, the chief addressed the matter at hand. "I understand you have some information pertaining to Dr. Fisk's death."

"Not—Not really," Laurel hedged. "The reporter twisted my words. I didn't say things the way she arranged them."

"I'm not referring to the so-called interview," the chief told her. "I'm referring to something Detective Resnick relayed to me, concerning the night Dr. Fisk was admitted to your ER. He tells me you have information that could be helpful."

Laurel shot a surprised glance in his direction. He stared straight ahead, his eyes resolutely on his superior.

Did this mean Cade believed her now? Or was he simply desperate enough to explore all options? From what she understood, they had no viable suspects in the case.

"I think it could be," she said slowly.

She went through the chain of events with the chief, encouraging Cade to offer his input on the matter. She was surprised when both men treated her as an equal, asking her opinion with genuine interest.

After almost an hour, the chief stood and extended his hand. "Thank you for coming in today, Miss Benson. I appreciate your input."

"Thank you, Chief Moore. I only want to see justice done."

"As do we all." He looked at his detective and tipped his chin. "Resnick, why don't you treat our guest to lunch? Use your expense account. It's the least we can do to repay her for her time and help this morning."

"Really, that isn't necessary..." Laurel protested.

"I'd join you, but I have another meeting." He said it as if it were the deciding factor in the matter.

"You heard the chief," Cade said, extending a hand to usher the way.

"Very well. Thank you, Chief Moore."

"My pleasure. If you think of anything else, keep Resnick informed."

As they walked stiffly down the hallway, Laurel hissed, "If I didn't know better, I'd think your chief was playing matchmaker!"

"Moore?" Cade asked in reply. "Never."

But as he pushed open the door, a tiny smile cracked his stony expression.

"Ride with me," Cade said when she would have headed toward her car. "I thought we'd try somewhere different today, and it's not that easy to find."

"Fine."

They were silent as they drove south out of town. After a few turns and winding roads, they wound up in a community so small, it didn't have a population count, simply a green road sign. A total of four buildings comprised the tiny town. There was a church, a gas station with a small convenience store, a rambling old building dubbed *His and Hers*, and *The Cafe* they sat in front of. The simple words were the only identification Laurel spotted, if she didn't count the assortment of vintage signs attached to the weathered exterior. If that were the case, it was Sinclair Gasoline, Iced Cold Coca-Cola Sold Here, Texaco Super Power Chief, 7Up, Coca-Cola in Bottles, Packard-Approved Service, Reddy Kilowatt Power Company, Smokey the Bear, Drink Dr. Pepper, Goodyear Tires, Clean Restrooms, US 66, King Edward's Cigars, Drink Mountain Dew—It will tickle your innards!, Dodge Brothers Sales and Service, red-winged flying horse.

I'm going with 'The Cafe,' she decided. Much easier to say when answering the phone.

When Cade opened the door, a bell jingled merrily above their heads. "After you," he invited.

"What is this place?" Laurel asked. She was immediately intrigued by the clean, simple decor, the mismatched tables and chairs scattered throughout the large space, and the tantalizing aromas floating on the air.

"The best food you've ever tasted," he told her with confidence.

A woman came toward them, her graying blonde hair escaping its messy bun, an apron sitting slightly askew upon her ample hips, and a genuine smile of pleasure lighting her face.

"Hey, sweetie," she greeted the detective. "This is an unexpected pleasure."

Laurel was surprised when Cade's tight face broke out

into a smile, and he bent to kiss the woman's cheek. "Hi, Mom."

Eyes wide, Laurel turned toward him with a question in her eyes.

Seeing the look, he shrugged. "What? I have parents. Pop's in the back, smoking the meat."

His mother chuckled. "He may act like it at times, but he wasn't raised by wolves." Her blue eyes twinkled as she settled her attention on Laurel. "And who do we have here?"

"Laurel Benson," she replied, extending a hand in greeting.

"Sandy Resnick," the other woman replied, wrapping both hands around Laurel's. "It's a pleasure to meet you. Usually, my son is too busy for lunch, so I appreciate anyone who can get him to stop long enough to eat."

"Mom," Cade said, stretching the word into a warning. "We're here to discuss a case."

"You're with the police department?" Mrs. Resnick asked in surprise.

"Actually, I'm a nurse."

"I always wanted to be a nurse," the sixty-something woman mused. "It would have come in handy, too, with my brood. Especially this one." She hitched a thumb toward her son and shook her head affectionately. "He was like an accident waiting to happen. Always skinning his knee, falling out of trees, or getting tangled up in barbed wire and ropes. Now he dodges bullets and chases criminals." She shook her head again, setting free another sprig of hair.

"We're going to our table now, Mom," Cade said, his voice endearingly indulgent. He took Laurel's elbow and guided her toward the far windows.

Impressed by the small lake they overlooked and the

green pastures beyond, Laurel smiled. "I had no idea your parents owned a cafe. In fact, I had no idea you had parents."

"Like Mom said, I wasn't raised by wolves."

"Where are we, anyway? I don't recognize the name of the town."

"It's more of a community, than a town. I was born and raised here. Still live nearby, actually."

"Really? I thought you lived on a ranch."

With a roll of the hand, he indicated the pastures beyond.

"This is yours?" Laurel asked in surprise.

"My family's, at any rate."

"Impressive." Her expression said it all.

A pretty waitress with long, brown hair plaited into a single braid pranced over to the table. "Hey, Cade," she said in singsong. "Long time, no see."

"Hey, Tori."

"What can I get you today? Your usual?"

Cade looked at Laurel with a devilish smile that took her breath away. "How hungry are you?"

She shrugged. "I can eat."

Cade looked back at the waitress who had yet to acknowledge his guest. "This is my friend Laurel. Bring us both the family special."

"I know you want your mama's sweet tea," Tori grinned. The smile fell when she finally turned to Laurel. "And you?"

"The same, please."

As Tori sashayed off with a swing in her hips, Laurel teased, "Somebody's got a crush." Seeing Cade in his natural surroundings made it impossible to stay mad at him. He looked so much more relaxed here. Not at all like a man who would hang up on her in anger and accuse her of selling him out.

Noting his reaction to her words, she laughed aloud. "To be a detective, you aren't very observant!"

Cade frowned. "She's like eighteen."

"She's twenty-two, if she's a day," Laurel argued. "And by the way, there's no age limit on crushes."

His frown lingered as he stared after the waitress. "Now I'm going to feel weird around her."

Laurel laughed at his predicament. "I know this isn't the first time this has happened to you."

"But Tori? I taught her how to ride horses when she was like six years old." He still looked disturbed by the thought of the young woman being attracted to him.

"Did we come here to discuss your throng of admirers?" Laurel wanted to know.

"No. We came here because this is the only place I knew where we could talk freely and not be disturbed."

As Tori threw back her shoulders and pranced back toward their table, Laurel grinned. "Lover girl didn't get the memo."

Cade grabbed her hand across the table and threaded his fingers through hers. Feeling her stiffen, he begged, "Play along."

Just a few days ago, their entwined fingers felt so right. Now it felt forced.

Maybe she hadn't let go of quite all her anger, after all.

Their clasped hands didn't escape the waitress' notice. Tori delivered their mason jars of tea with a thud. When she flounced off without a word, Laurel knew his ploy had worked.

"I want you to know that I took your advice," Cade told her, holding her hand steadfast when she tried tugging it free. "I took a step back from the case, looked at it objectively, and discovered a few things that warranted a closer look. I'm still not sold on your superpower to decipher mumbo-jumbo, but a lot of what you said made sense. As of today, ACAF is under investigation. I wanted you to know first."

Laurel was surprised—and flattered—that he had taken her advice, even more so that he admitted to it. "Is that what the meeting with the chief was about?" He confirmed with a nod. "Can you tell me anything more?"

He continued to play with her fingers, absently rubbing the ring she wore.

"It's true that ACAF has had more than one extramarital affair over the years. Rumor has it he wasn't exactly faithful, himself, but nothing has been confirmed. To my knowledge, once they moved here to the twin cities, they've been monogamous to one another."

Laurel pursed her lips. "Then how do you explain the slippers?"

"I can't. And just because I don't know about any affairs doesn't mean they haven't existed. Maybe they've just managed to keep a low profile."

"Which is odd, considering that despite a population of close to three hundred thousand and growing, Bryan-College Station still has that everyone-knows-everyone mentality."

"Try growing up here," Cade said, flashing that devastating smile again as he tilted his head toward the window. He rocked their hands on the table. "The rumor mill will have us engaged by nightfall."

Her hazel eyes twinkled playfully. "We're holding hands in your mama's cafe, after all," she joked.

She felt him start to pull away, but then he stopped himself. When he gave her hand a gentle squeeze, her heart jingled in her chest.

Get a grip, girl, she cautioned herself. You're not

thirteen.

"Is it true," Laurel asked, struggling to maintain a steady voice and to pull her mind back to the case, "that she had an affair with a known criminal?"

"That's still a little hazy. There were accusations, but no real proof. I tend to think it had more to do with her brother, than with her."

"The one who came to the hospital with her?"

"I think he's the only one she has. I've done a little digging on him, but so far, I haven't found much. But something about him feels a little off."

"Off? Like mental problems?" she questioned.

"Maybe. But more like drug problems. He seemed particularly nervous. Very agitated."

"Yes, but from what I understand, he and Dr. Fisk were like best friends. They did everything together. I'm sure he was in shock, seeing him like that."

Cade shrugged his broad shoulders and mused, "Maybe. But there was something about him that didn't sit right with me. And ACAF has made comments about him, here and there. She's taken a hard stance on drug abuse, citing family experience. He came to live with them about two years ago, after traveling a long and twisted road. He seems to be on the straight and narrow now, but in my experience, it seldom lasts. Let's hope this time is the exception."

Their first course arrived, forcing their hands apart. Sandy Resnick beamed with delight as she noted their hasty shuffling. She balanced a tray on the table to deliver cups of thick, steaming-hot chicken and dumplings and a basket of small cornbread muffins.

Laurel inhaled the mouth-watering aromas. "This looks and smells delicious."

"Go easy on the portions," Cade warned. "There's

plenty more to come."

And come, it did. The family special turned out to be a sampler's feast of practically everything on the menu, and then some. By the time Laurel pushed the last plate away, she was miserably, delightedly stuffed.

"I cannot believe I ate all that," she said in wonder. "That had to be the best brisket I've ever put in my mouth."

"Pop is the pit master," Cade said, the pride evident in his voice. "He gets up every morning at five a.m. to stoke the fire in the pit, even when it's a hundred and five outside."

"He is definitely a master."

"I'll take you out back to meet him."

"You mean you'll roll me out. I don't think I can even move right now."

He chuckled at her exaggeration, which was no exaggeration at all. "We'll sit for a little while longer," he agreed.

This new, relaxed Cade intrigued Laurel. "You don't have to get back to the precinct?"

"Hey, I have the chief's blessing," he reminded her. "Besides, I'm working here."

"On a piece of apple cobbler," she snickered. "What is that? Your third dessert?"

"Don't think I didn't notice you had the banana pudding *and* the kolache."

"But it was poppy seed, my favorite. And it was divine."

Cade nodded. "My grandmother makes them. From scratch."

Laurel grinned. "Is there any other way?"

"Not in my family. Boxed mixes are heavily frowned upon."

When Cade's phone buzzed, he winced and said, "I need to take this. I silenced everything but the chief. This is him."

"Go. I understand."

"I'll just be a minute."

Laurel watched his slim silhouette move against the glare of the window and disappear out the back door. As he paced close to the water, his phone in one hand and the back of his neck gripped in the other, Laurel knew the conversation wasn't going well. She absently reached over and stole a bite of his cobbler. Like everything else, it was delicious.

Sandy wandered over to her table with a smile. Seeing her son pacing in the yard, she tipped her head toward him. "He's a dedicated lawman, you know."

Laurel smiled. "Yes, I know."

"In fact, he's loyal and dedicated to everything that's important to him." Her voice fell as she added softly, "That applies to people, too."

Laurel tried not to frown. He had doubted *her*, though. Did that mean she wasn't important to him?

"It's been a long time since he's brought a woman in, you know," Sandy added with a sly smile. "It's good to see that smile on his face again."

"Oh, we're just—" She stopped, not sure exactly *what* they were.

"Let me guess. It's complicated, right?"

A sigh escaped her. "And then some," Laurel admitted.

"I used to think the same thing about my James. But then one day, I realized it was all quite simple. He completed me. After that, the complications were more like little hiccups. Every relationship has them."

"I'm not sure we have a relationship." Laurel was

surprised at how much it hurt to admit that.

Sandy gave her an amused smile. Her eyes traveled outside to her son, who had paused in his conversation to look up at Laurel, sitting there in the window. He didn't even notice his mother by her side.

"You have a relationship," Sandy informed her. "Don't let a hiccup or two stand in your way."

As Cade put away his phone and started back toward the building, Laurel smiled. "Thank you, Mrs. Resnick. It's been a pleasure meeting you. And the meal was absolutely amazing."

"I like to give first timers and family a little taste of everything. Next time, you can go with just one, if you like. And the next, you can have something else." She winked and added, "I have a feeling you'll be coming back often."

Laurel watched Cade stomp his feet clean and make his way toward her. Her heart did that jingle thing again. "I hope so," she confided to his mother.

"Uh-oh," Cade said in mock horror. "I know that look. Has Mom been telling stories about my childhood, again? Anything too embarrassingly personal?"

"Not at all," Laurel assured him with a laugh. "She was just giving me a home remedy for hiccups."

"O—kay," he said skeptically, his brown eyes darting between the two laughing women. He offered Laurel his hand. "Ready to meet the pit master?"

"I think I can move now." When her feet felt sluggish and her legs heavy, she added, "Maybe."

Cade slid an arm around her small waist. "You can lean on me."

James Resnick was an older, more mature version of his son and every bit as handsome. First impressions told her he was more amiable and much more laid back. If today was any indication, however, there was hope for Cade yet.

It's the pressures of his job, she decided as they walked back to his truck and climbed inside. Like me, he has a lot of responsibility, and a lot of people depending on him. And just like me, it's often a life and death situation.

"That was wonderful. Thank you for bringing me," she told him as she buckled up.

"Mom refuses to let me pay, so, technically, I still owe you a meal on the department's dime," he informed her. "Maybe another day this week?"

"I'm off until Thursday."

"Wednesday, then?"

"Wednesday, it is."

As they wound their way back toward the city limits, Cade told her about the phone call. "The chief called to give me an update. Effective immediately, ACAF is on administrative leave, pending further investigation. Publicly, he's calling it bereavement absence, but she knows she's considered a suspect."

"I wish I were wrong about what I heard, Cade," Laurel told him softly.

A muscle worked along his jaw. The closer they got to College Station, the tighter he was wound.

"You're absolutely certain of what you heard?"

Laurel puffed out a breath and thought carefully about her answer. "I'm sure of the inflection. I'm sure of the pacing of the words. I'm sure of the number of syllables. I'm sure of the urgency in his voice."

She closed her eyes and recalled the exact sounds he uttered.

"*Na*. No. *Na-nin-na*. Three syllables, like Corinda. *Nun nus*. Two syllables, two words. Did this. *Ha nun nus*.

Three words, almost in panic. She did this." Laurel opened her eyes and nodded in certainty. "She came near his bedside, and he wanted us to know that she had done this to him. I'm sorry, Cade, but I believe your boss is guilty. I think she regrets it now because she did love him, but I think she attacked her husband in a fit of passion and rage."

Cade considered the physical probability of her claim. "He outweighed her by a good sixty pounds. He was taller, too."

"He was out of shape and flabby," Laurel contradicted. "He sat behind a desk all day. As a police officer, she's strong enough. Fit enough. It's what she's trained to do."

Laurel reached out a hand to take his across the seat. "I'm sorry, Cade," she said softly.

"I am, too."

CHAPTER TWELVE

Arnold Fisk's funeral was held on Wednesday morning. It seemed the whole community mourned as hundreds of people poured into the church to pay their respects.

Cade attended in his dress blues, sitting with his fellow officers in a show of unison and support for their assistant chief. Out of respect for their superior and for the belief in 'innocent until proved guilty,' the investigation was confined to and conducted by select detectives. The rest believed the grieving widow was taking a leave of absence, and the stories originally aired by WXZY (and since taken down) were nothing but sensational journalism.

Going for a late lunch after the funeral was over, Laurel was thrilled to be in the presence of such a handsome and distinguished-looking date. In truth, she would be thrilled to be with Cade even if he were dressed in rags. But a uniform never hurt.

"Now what?" Laurel asked.

"We'll keep looking into ACAF's past and talk to the people who knew her best. Surprisingly enough, she hadn't made very many friends here in Aggieland yet."

"Even after four years?" Laurel was dubious.

"According to her, they were building their careers

and rebuilding their marriage. Then her brother moved here, and much of their time was dedicated to getting him back on his feet. I'm reaching out to former colleagues in Chicago and Little Rock, but it's a slow process. No one is under obligation to speak with me."

"I know you can't tell me, but I don't suppose you found any incriminating fingerprints? Or the shoe, itself?"

"If I could tell you, it would be to say that there's nothing remarkable about any of the evidence we've gathered thus far. No prints that shouldn't be there. And no shoe."

"And Rita Bernard? Did she check out?"

"What do you mean?"

Laurel shrugged. "I keep wondering if she's the one Dr. Fisk was having an affair with."

"She did seem to take his death extremely hard," Cade agreed, "but I don't think there was anything going on between them." A frown puckered his lips. "Don't read anything into this, because everyone shows and feels grief in their own way, but the AC was taking it better than any of the immediate family and friends. The daughter, the brother-in-law, and the secretary were all a basketcase, while she held herself together stoically."

"I agree," Laurel murmured, "that it doesn't mean anything. Grief affects everyone differently. But no tears?"

"Of course she cried some, but nothing like her brother. I don't think I've ever seen a man cry that much. The oddest thing was that when I went to pay my respects, she kept mumbling something about smelling the roses and blowing out candles."

A smile hovered on Laurel's lips. "Not so odd. It's a relaxation technique, targeted to control one's breathing.

I showed it to her in the ER."

"She put it to good use today."

"Back to the secretary. Or, I should say, the administrative assistant. If she took his death so hard, why don't you think she could have been having an affair with her boss? It seems to happen quite often. And she does have a large foot."

"I don't think she's of the same persuasion as the doctor," he offered.

"What do you—" Her eyes widened, but then her shoulders slumped. "Oh." It had seemed like a good lead. Changing the subject, she said, "Speaking of such, did you know there's a gay bar in Northgate called *Rainbow Bridge*?"

"As a matter of fact, I do know it. It's not the only one, either. I've had occasion to visit most of them more than once."

Laurel pretended to pout. "Should I be worried? Are you telling me my competition wears beards?"

His brown eyes twinkled in jest. "I make it a point to never date a woman with a beard. The very first present I give her is always a razor."

"Good to know."

Cade reached across the table to run his fingers along her cheek. "Just a little peach fuzz," he reported. "I think you'll be good."

Laurel laughed aloud. "Thanks for that. I think."

His fingers lingered before slowly falling away. Laurel's heart jingled like spinning spurs.

"When do I get to see you rope?"

"Where did that come from?" He gave a half-laugh. "Isn't that sort of out of the blue?"

She wasn't about to explain the analogy between her heartbeat and how he looked in spurs and cowboy attire.

Or how he looked in his dress blues. Or in his detective clothes. Or even in those rags she had imagined. She was in real danger of falling for this man, and she doubted it would be pretty. More like a skid-on-her-knees and land-on-her-face sort of fall. The kind she would never quite recover from.

"Laurel?" he asked in concern. "Where did you go? I lost you for a second."

"Uhm, sorry. Just thinking."

"Thinking about *my* competition?" he teased. "Not someone you met at Northgate, I hope."

"Well," Laurel pretended to ponder the question, "I did have a moment with a guy in drag, but I don't think you need to worry. I don't care much for purple, and he wore it from head to toe."

"Yeah, not a look I can pull off," he agreed.

"That's okay. I like cowboy hats. So." She drummed her fingers against the tabletop. "About that roping…"

"First, we're having that date."

"When?" She didn't worry about sounding too eager. She was eager.

"I don't know. I'm off the next two days, then work the weekend."

"My schedule is the exact opposite."

"Monday?"

"Working."

"Me, too."

"That's the week of Thanksgiving," she pointed out. "If either of us showed up at the other's family function, both our mothers would start printing wedding invitations."

Cade flashed an apologetic smile. "My grandmother sent a message to say you were invited on Turkey Day."

Laurel let out a burst of laughter that doubled as a

moan. "Wow. You weren't kidding. Word travels fast. And it's just as bad in my family. No offense, but I don't want you anywhere near me on Thanksgiving, or they'll have us married off by Christmas Day."

"No offense taken. I agree completely. So. First week of December?"

"I'll pencil you in."

"No." Cade's voice was firm. "We're using a permanent marker."

With Thanksgiving a week away, Laurel started early on her baking. She only had a few days off between now and then, and she wanted to make the most of her time. She had signed up to make the cornbread dressing this year, so she spent the weekend stirring up multiple batches of cornbread, baking them to golden perfection, and storing them in her freezer.

She was waiting for the last batch to come out of the oven when her doorbell rang. Cami had mentioned she might drop by. Thinking it was her friend, Laurel wiped her hands on a dishrag and went to the door.

"M—M—Mrs. Fisk," she said in surprise. "What—What are you doing here?"

"I realize this is highly unusual. And probably a bit uncomfortable," the other woman apologized, wringing her hands nervously. "I went by the hospital, but they told me you had the day off. And—And I really wanted to talk with you. May I come in?"

Laurel debated on how to answer. On the one hand, the woman seemed genuinely distressed. *The same way she had probably been when she stabbed her husband in the heart*, a little voice said in Laurel's head. On the other hand, it went against her Southern breeding to be so rude as to deny a guest, even though uninvited.

She shifted on her feet, caught in a silent tug of war. Good hostess, or potential next victim? Hear what the woman had to say, or assume the worst of her?

In the end, good manners and curiosity won out.

"Come in," she said, pulling the door open wider and hoping she didn't live to regret it. *Dying regretting it would be worse*, she reminded herself.

"I won't stay long," Corinda Addison-Fisk promised. "But I need your help."

"How?"

"I keep having panic attacks," she admitted. She shrugged out of her coat and helped herself to a seat on the couch.

Okay, not at all threatening. Everything will be fine.

Realizing she waited on a response, Laurel scrambled to keep up. "I'm sorry to hear that. But how can I help?"

"Will you breathe with me again?"

"Of course."

Laurel took a seat across from her visitor and reached for her hands. She noticed Mrs. Fisk still wore her wedding ring, something that seemed odd for a killer to do.

"I don't know what's wrong with me," the woman confessed. "My daughter has gone home, and now I just feel so… lost. So alone. All I seem to do is cry and have these panic attacks. It's embarrassing."

"Why should that be embarrassing? It's a perfectly normal response to grieving."

After several breathing exercises, Corinda calmed down and ducked her head. "Thank you. You've been very kind to me. Considering."

A ripple of unease slid down Laurel's spine, especially

when her guest shot her a covert glance. "Considering?"

"I heard the interview. I know it was edited, but I also know…" She lifted her head and looked her directly in the eye. "You think I'm guilty, don't you?"

"I, uh, wouldn't exactly say that," Laurel hedged. She shifted her legs, arranging them for a faster getaway, should it come to that.

"You were there that night. You were the nurse. Did he—Did he say anything? Did he talk to you?"

Is this a trap? Laurel wondered. *She looks rather desperate, but is she desperate to know the truth, or desperate to keep the truth to herself?*

"It keeps me awake at night," the widow continued, "wondering if he knew what happened to him. Wondering if he was in tremendous pain, or if he was too numbed and incoherent to know the difference." She sniffed into a handkerchief and *darned if it didn't look convincing.* Laurel felt conflicted, torn between pity and suspicion.

"What if he tried to give me a message, and I didn't know? What if—what if he knew his killer, and he's out there, walking free, and I do nothing to stop it? They suspended me, you know. They won't let me help with the case. They won't tell me a thing!"

Is that why she's here? She thinks I'm responsible for her suspension? Which I guess I am, in a way, but that's no reason for her to come here and get revenge.

Inspiration hit. "Would you like me to call Detective Resnick? I'm sure he would come right over and bring you up to speed on the case."

Instead of agreeing, she frowned. "I don't think that's a good idea."

"You—You don't?"

"No. He might think I was harassing you. That I

came here to harm you in some way."

Laurel gulped and dared to ask, "Did you?"

Corinda looked genuinely aghast. "What? Why would I do that? You've been nothing but kind to me! And... And you were one of the last people to help my Arnold. I don't think he ever regained consciousness after surgery. Yours could be the last face he saw."

"I'm certain he knew when you and your brother arrived."

"How can you be sure? That's what tortures me. That he may not know I was there with him."

"Oh, he knew."

Corinda looked at her strangely, but before Laurel had to explain her remarks, the timer on the oven sounded.

"I'm sorry, but I have something in the oven. Are you feeling better now?"

"Much. Thank you." She smiled but didn't take the hint to leave.

The buzzer continued to wail.

"My cornbread..."

"Don't let me stop you. Go. Take care of it before it burns."

Laurel stood, shifting from one foot to another. "If there's nothing else I can do for you..."

"Actually, there is something else..."

Uh-oh. The unease slid further over her.

"Mrs. Fisk, I really don't think..."

The smell of crispy cornbread filled the air. Her oven had been overheating lately. Any minute now, the smoke alarm would go off, and the cornbread would burn. She would have to start over, and she was out of cornmeal.

"Please excuse me," she said hurriedly, making a decision. She made a dash for the kitchen, grabbing her phone as she went. She would call Cade from the other room.

And with any luck, Cami would drop by, too. In fact, was that the doorbell she heard?

Relief washed over her, knowing reinforcement had arrived.

"Could you get the door, please?" Laurel called, turning off the oven and pulling a double batch of crispy-edged cornbread from the rack. She fanned away a hazy puff of smoke and listened for the cheerful lilt of Cami's voice.

"Cami, I'm in the kitchen. Come on back!"

She heard footsteps, but when she turned, it wasn't her friend. Corinda stood there, looking unsure of herself.

"It, uh, wasn't who you thought," the woman said.

"Who was it? A delivery?"

"Not—Not exactly. It was, uhm, it was—" Corinda looked oddly upset, her voice hesitant. "It was my brother."

Perplexed, Laurel looked beyond her first visitor as another stepped into view. Both were unexpected and, frankly, unwelcomed. Not that it had stopped either from barging in.

"H—Hello?" she offered hesitantly.

Six foot even, slender build, but good muscle tone and sinewy muscle. Could be guilty of steroid abuse, but probably not hard drugs. His eyes, though, do look a bit glazed. Appears fidgety and nervous, like Cade said. Could be in early stages of drug dependency.

"Yeah, hey," the man said distractedly. He acted as if Laurel had wandered randomly into his home, not the other way around. "I, uhm, was looking for my sister."

"And now you've found her!" Laurel inserted extra enthusiasm into her voice, eager to have these people gone. "And this cornbread isn't going to pop itself out of the pan, so I'll see you both to the door."

"Nah, I could go for a piece of cornbread with a nice big slather of butter on it." His eyes hungrily wandered to the pan.

How rude!

Employing a different tactic, Laurel smiled brightly and held the just-from-the-oven pan toward him. The hot metal burned through the thin hot pads she held it with, but she would walk over hot coals to have these people out of her house.

"You know what? I never brought a meal over to the house after the funeral. Please, accept this pan of cornbread."

"I can eat it here."

"Benji, you're being rude!" Corinda hissed. She offered Laurel a weak smile. "Thank you all the same, Nurse Benson, but we'll be leaving now."

Benji turned to his sister and all but screamed, "Would you stop mothering me! I'm not a little kid. I know what I want. And I want cornbread."

"Then, let's take it home and eat it there. I'll get you some milk to go with it, just like Mama used to do." She tugged on his arm, but he shook it loose.

"I'm hungry. I want it now." He sounded like a stubborn child.

Corinda sent Laurel a silent, desperate message with her eyes. The man had issues. He could be volatile and possibly dangerous. It was best to play along and appease him.

"I'll see if I have milk," Laurel offered, turning toward the refrigerator. With her back turned, she could send Cade a message.

"No," the big man decided. "You stay where you are.

Sister will get it."

Laurel felt like a hostage in her own home even though, to her knowledge, neither intruder had a weapon. That had to count for something. Right?

"I'll get butter, too," Corinda said, keeping her voice pleasant and soothing. "Then I thought we might stop by the Dairy Queen and get one of those dipped cones you like so much. That would be good. Right, Benji?"

"Getting too cold for ice cream." The man's anxiety ratcheted up, and he began to pace. Not large to begin with, the kitchen felt cramped with the three of them in it, especially with one of them mumbling to himself and walking back and forth at an increasingly frantic pace.

"She told you," he muttered. "She told you what I did." He seemed to speak to himself, saying the words over and over, until he finally lifted his head and shouted to Laurel. "I'm talking to you! She told you, didn't she?"

"T—Told me what?"

"What I did."

"I honestly have no idea what you're talking about," Laurel said honestly.

"Then why is she here?"

"I was helping her with some breathing exercises."

"I don't believe you! She already knows how to breathe!" he accused.

"It's a relaxation technique. Here, I'll show you. Let's do this together." Laurel inched closer, hoping to make a personal connection with him. "Start by taking a deep, cleansing breath. Imagine that you're breathing in a beautiful red rose."

"I don't like roses!"

"Okay, okay. Then... breathe in the cornbread. Think of how good it's going to taste. Take a deep whiff of all that deliciousness. But it's going to be hot. You need to blow on it to cool it off. So, breathe in slowly, and blow out quickly. You try it," she encouraged.

He gave up after only two repetitions. "This is stupid. I don't want to smell cornbread; I want to eat it!"

"Here. Here, Benji." His sister hurried over with a nice, big piece. "It's a corner, just as you like. Try that. It looks delicious, doesn't it?" As she placed it in front of him, she turned to Laurel, her eyes sad and worried. Silently, she mouthed, "I'm so sorry."

Laurel tried to decipher the family dynamics. Benji was the younger of the two and was either mentally disturbed or had fried his mind with too many drugs. Corinda had probably helped raise him and still tended to baby him, trying to act as a buffer between his fragile state and the harsh realities of life. She brought him here to live with her, hoping to help him, even though he was a grown man and responsible for his own choices in life, however poor they might be. Laurel would wager to say he was capable of knowing right from wrong; he seemed to be more of a spoiled brat than anything else. His sister was clearly frightened of him and what he might do, meaning he was a wild card.

"It's good, don't you think?" Laurel asked, trying again to engage with him. "Do you like to bake, Benji?"

"No. But I like to eat."

"Don't we all."

He polished off the cornbread, stuffing huge chunks into his mouth. He washed it down with milk, allowing the liquid to dribble down his chin. Laurel questioned her earlier assessment. Maybe this man truly did have a mental disability. In that case, he needed professional help.

"I have a friend I'd like you to meet, Benji. Would you mind if I called her and asked her to come over?"

"Don't do that!" He pounded his fist on the top of the butcherblock bar, causing his empty plate to clatter and jump.

The women in the room did the same.

"Okay. Sure. I won't call," Laurel agreed.

He cast an accusing gaze her way. "You know who I am, don't you?"

She slid an uneasy glance toward his sister. "Yes," Laurel agreed slowly, fearing anything she said might set him off. "You're Benji. Corinda's brother."

"You know who I am. You're following me. You came to the hospital. And you saw me that night."

"I'm a nurse, Benji. I work at the hospital. That's the only place I've ever seen you."

"No. You saw me. You ran into me. You ran into me at the *Rainbow Bridge*."

CHAPTER THIRTEEN

Could it be? Could Benji have been the man she saw coming out of the bar?

The man had seemed vaguely familiar that night. He had stared at her so strangely. Something like recognition had mingled in his eyes, swirling with defiance and an attempt at sobriety. But the man had been dressed in drag, and...

And nothing. She knew nothing about Benji, not even his last name. Of course, it could have been him. Not that it mattered to Laurel.

Obviously, however, it mattered to Benji.

She tried for an easy smile. "I think I have that kind of face. People think they've met me before because I have such a generic look."

"Don't mess with me. I'm not stupid!" One swipe of his hand, and the plate sailed off the bar and shattered on the floor.

"Of—Of course not. I'll just get a broom and clean that up."

"No. You'll sit here in this chair, and you'll stay there, until I tell you to get up! You, too, Rinda. I need to think."

As both women did as told, he paced again, back and forth across the floor.

Out of nowhere, he whirled and accused his sister, "You cheated on him, Rinda! How could you have done that to him? Arnie was a good man. He was the best." Tears streamed down his face now. "He was my best friend. He was my soulmate. I loved him. Do you hear me, Rinda? I loved him!" The big man shouted at her, pounding on his chest where the aching void must have been.

"Yes, Benji, I know you did. And he loved you. We both did. You were always welcome in our home."

"But you cheated on him! You didn't love him!"

"Yes, I did. I did love him, more than you could imagine. But ours was a different kind of marriage. We weren't like other married couples, but we loved each other deeply."

"Not enough. Not enough," he chanted, continuing to pace. "You didn't love him enough. He loved you too much. But it wasn't enough. Not enough."

"Let's go home, Benji, where we can talk about this."

"Sit down! I told you to sit down!" He paced along the counter, and suddenly there was a knife in his hand. He swiped it from the knife block, brandishing the wide blade in the air.

"Rabenja Elijah!" his sister chastised. "You put that down!"

"I'm not a child anymore, Rinda. You can't tell me what to do!" He stuck his chin out stubbornly, just like a four-year-old.

Okay, I was wrong. Serious mental issues, with or without drug use.

"You know what I did," Benji said. "I can see it in your eyes. You found out."

His sister hung her head, shaking it slowly back and forth. "After all we did for you. We took you in, Benji.

Again. We tried to give you a fresh start, here in a new place." Her voice reflected her heartbreak. "But you started using again. I found his checkbook when I cleaned out his office."

Laurel's eyes widened. *Is that what she meant when she said it was her fault? I thought she was confessing to murder!*

Corinda looked up, her black eyes bright with unshed tears. "You were blackmailing him, weren't you? After all we did for you, you took advantage of Arnold's goodness. You knew something, and you used it against him so he would keep you in drugs."

"He kept me, all right," Benji spat. "And I knew plenty."

A new memory came to mind about Corinda's visit to the ER. She said she had brought him here. She meant her brother? She found out about the blackmail and blamed herself for bringing him back into their lives? That's what she meant?

"Why, Benji? Why did you do it?" Corinda wanted to know.

"Because you kept cheating on him! You didn't deserve him."

"I told you. Our situation was different. I know you don't understand…"

"I understand everything, big sister. And I understood Arnie like you never could." He pounded his chest again, with the hand not holding the knife. "We were just alike. Do you hear me? Just. Alike."

She looked at him in confusion, until something finally dawned in her eyes. She took in a sharp breath and looked away from his accusing glare.

"You really didn't know, did you?" His laugh was hollow. "You never knew I was gay."

Laurel's head whipped around in surprise, sending her dark curls flying. She darted her gaze between the two siblings. *Okay, so that could have been Benji in drag.*

"I—I'm sorry," Corinda said, the tears now flowing down her face. "I didn't know. But it wouldn't have mattered. I would have loved you anyway. Just like I loved Arnold."

Wait. What? Laurel struggled to keep up with the conversation. *Surely, she's not saying what I think she's saying.*

His next words confirmed it. "You didn't care that your husband was gay? You loved him anyway?" he taunted.

"Yes! And he loved me. We—We didn't share a bedroom, not that way, but we shared everything else. Somehow, it worked for us."

This is getting weirder by the minute. And somehow, it's all playing out in my kitchen.

"Except it wasn't working anymore, big sister. There was someone else in his life. Someone he loved as much as he loved you. Maybe even more."

"No. That's not true. How would you even know that?"

Now is a good time for me to duck out. This sounds like a family matter. They won't even know I'm gone. Staying crouched over, Laurel slipped from her seat. Neither sibling noticed.

Benji laughed again, the sound bitter and cruel. "You really are stupid, you know that? You don't know, do you?" He came closer with the knife, waving it in front of him as his voice grew louder. "You really don't know, you stupid, selfish, self-centered cow!"

"What are talking about, Rabenja?" she snapped.

"We weren't just best friends. All those days and

nights we spent in his man cave, just the two of us. We weren't watching football, you dumb broad. We were lovers! We have been for almost two years, right beneath your nose! And we were in love. Do you hear me? We. Were. In. Love." He pounded his chest again, roaring like a lion.

Corinda wasn't the only one who hadn't seen it coming. As his sister gasped in shocked horror, Laurel's head snapped backward to the raging man. She made a misstep, crunching down on a piece of the broken plate and drawing his attention back to her.

"Sit your skinny butt down!" he hissed.

Laurel gulped and did as she was told. She could see the madness in his eyes now. The man was coming unhinged.

A terrible thought occurred to her. *Rabenja.* The same number of syllables as Corinda. The same cadence. The same inflection. The same accusation.

But. A different name.

How could I have been so wrong? Laurel was horrified by her mistake. She had accused an innocent woman of murder! More than that, she had accused a loving wife of killing her husband. And she had convinced Cade to believe the worst of his superior.

Without thinking, Laurel's eyes flew to Benji's feet. Yep. An easy size twelve. And the man was definitely a drag queen.

"What are you looking at?" he screamed. "You know, don't you? That's why you've been following me! You know!" He waved the knife in her face, coming so close, she could hear it cut through the very air she breathed. She drew back, stifling a gasp of fear.

Corinda had dropped her head onto her arms and wept with the realization of her husband and brother's betrayal, but she pulled her head up now, staring at the deranged man in even more horror and disbelief.

"What did you do?" she asked coldly.

When he didn't answer, she repeated the question, her voice building with a quiet and deadly calm. "Rabenja. What. Did. You. Do."

A light of panic moved into his crazed eyes. "He—He was breaking up with me. He said he still loved you. He was choosing you, over me. But I was his soulmate. Me!"

He advanced toward his sister, spittle flying from his mouth as he yelled the angry words.

Undaunted, Corinda rose from her chair and assumed a warrior's stance. She was no longer afraid of her brother.

"Do you hear me, big sister? I was his soulmate. I wasn't going to let him leave me like that. I was his soulmate. Me! Just me!" He pounded his chest again, his fist pumping with anger and passion and every ounce of love he had felt for the man.

But in his rage, he used the wrong hand.

It happened fast after that, but it seemed to play out in slow motion. The knife sank into his chest. In his deranged state of mind, he didn't feel the pain. He jerked the knife out and stabbed it in again with the next vehemently bellowed, "Me!"

This time, it lodged in his breastbone. Benji gurgled, staring down in confusion at the bright red bloom of color on his chest. Red. Like the roses Arnie always gave to *her*, not him.

He bellowed again in rage, but he was falling. The weight of his body forced the blade in deeper.

"Call 9-1-1!" Laurel shouted, her training kicking in. She stripped off her sweater, flipped him over onto his back with inhuman strength, and started chest compressions. "Not again," she moaned. She looked at the stricken woman beside her. "Corinda! Call 9-1-1."

The policewoman's voice was cold and flat. "He killed Arnold. Let him die."

"Not on my watch!" Laurel roared. "And not on my floor. Call 9-1-1. *Now!*" She barked out the order in a voice that brooked no argument. "And call Cade. His number is in my phone."

Laurel continued chest compressions, her arms aching and sweat dripping from her face, while Corinda placed the calls. Snapping slowly from her daze, the devastated widow took turns spelling Laurel until the paramedics arrived.

"How could I have been so wrong?" Laurel sobbed as the medics took over. She turned to Corinda and apologized for the umpteenth time. "I'm so sorry."

Corinda wrapped her arms around her and cried along with her. They had both been so wrong about so many things.

The ambulance left with the unconscious man as Cade arrived. Laurel collapsed into his arms, her heart as bruised and tortured as her body.

"I was wrong, Cade. I was so horribly wrong."

Cade pushed the limp curls from her face and kissed her forehead. "You may have an awesome superpower, but you're still human. Everyone makes mistakes now and then."

"But mistakes aren't allowed in my profession. Or in yours."

"We're all human, Laurel. Sooner or later, we all make mistakes, whether they're allowed or not. It's inevitable."

"I could have ruined her life. Her career. I was such an idiot! I was so sure of myself. So arrogant and —"

"Hey. Let's get something straight." Cade put a finger

to her chin and lifted her tear-streaked face to his. "For the first time in a very long time, I've found a woman I'm interested in, and I happen to think she's pretty terrific. I won't have you talking trash about her."

"She's such a mess right now."

"She's the most exciting, beautiful, passionate mess I've seen in forever," he told her with a smile. "And even though I'm not going to spend Thanksgiving Day with her, we have our first date scheduled for soon after. And who knows? If it goes well, we may give Christmas a try."

"That—That sounds awfully ambitious, don't you think?"

"I prefer to think of it as challenging."

"Let's start with that dinner, shall we?"

"Sounds like a plan." The smile faded from his eyes, and he sighed heavily. "But first, we need to go down to the precinct. I have to take your official statement."

Benji survived surgery and was remanded to a psychiatric hospital for a complete and extended evaluation. He would likely spend the rest of his life in confinement.

With her dignity and her position fully intact, Corinda resigned from the College Station Police Department. She returned to Chicago to be near her daughter, who was, indeed, Dr. Fisk's biological child. Corinda had never been involved with a drug lord, other than interaction forced by her brother.

Thanksgiving came and went, celebrated with their respective families, but on the first Tuesday in December, Cade and Laurel went on their long-awaited 'official' first date. They didn't take the chance on waiting for a weekend when their schedules coincided; he booked the restaurant's first available table.

They didn't talk about work. They didn't discuss patients or investigations. They talked about themselves and their interests. They concentrated on getting to know one another and discovering what they had in common, and what they didn't.

At the end of the evening, Cade walked Laurel to her door. A chill rode on the air, turning their cheeks rosy and their breaths frosty.

"Would you like to come in for hot cocoa?" she offered. "Or coffee?"

"Would I like to? Yes. Am I going to? No," he said with a rueful shake of his head. "It's been the perfect evening. Given our track record, I think we should quit while we're ahead."

"I think maybe you're right," Laurel agreed with a giggle.

As Cade moved in to kiss her, an odd burble worked its way up his diaphragm and pushed out on a hitch.

"Sorry about that," he said, clearly embarrassed. He moved in again, only to have it repeated.

Much to his chagrin, Cade discovered he had the hiccups. "I haven't had the hiccups in years," he muttered.

On the third try, they laughed. "Maybe I pushed my luck a little too far," he admitted. He eyed her in thought. "Didn't you say my mother told you about a home remedy for hiccups?"

Laurel's eyes twinkled. "As a matter of fact, she did."

"And? What was it?"

"I think," she said, stepping closer and reaching her arms up to encircle his neck, "it started with a kiss."

"Hey," Cade said, snagging her waist and pulling her close. "I think I like this approach to medicine."

"And if it doesn't work?" she murmured.

He lowered his face to hers. "We keep trying until it does."

Watch for more adventure with Laurel, Cade, and their College Station friends this summer. In the meantime, the two will make a guest appearance in the upcoming "Bye, Buy Baby," Book 11 of *The Sisters, Texas Mystery Series*, available March 2021.

Thank you so much for reading! I'm sorry to come begging, but if you enjoyed this story, please leave a review on Amazon, BookBub, Goodreads, or the site of your choice. Reviews make such a huge impact on a book's success!

You can also drop in a for an e-visit at beckiwillis.ccp@gmail.com or at www.beckiwillis.com. Hope to hear from you!

ABOUT THE AUTHOR

Best-selling indie author Becki Willis loves crafting stories with believable characters in believable situations. Many of her stories stem from her own travels and from personal experiences. (No worries; she's never actually murdered anyone).

When she's not plotting danger and adventure for her imaginary friends, Becki enjoys reading, antiquing (aka junking), unraveling a good mystery (real or imagined), dark chocolate, and a good cup of coffee. A professed history geek, Becki often weaves pieces of the past into her novels. Family is a central theme in her stories and in her life. She and her husband enjoy traveling, but believe coming home to their Texas ranch is the best part of any trip.

Becki has won numerous awards, but the real compliments come from her readers. Drop in for an e-visit anytime at beckiwillis.ccp@gmail.com, or www.beckiwillis.com.

Made in United States
North Haven, CT
26 May 2022